Finger Bone

HIROKI TAKAHASHI

Translated by Takami Nieda

Honford
Star

This translation first published by Honford Star 2023

Honford Star Ltd.
Profolk, Bank Chambers
Stockport
SK1 1AR
honfordstar.com

YUBI NO HONE
by Hiroki Takahashi
Copyright © 2015 Hiroki Takahashi
All rights reserved.
Original Japanese edition published by SHINCHOSA Publishing Co., Ltd. in 2015
English translation rights arranged with SHINCHOSA Publishing Co., Ltd.
through Japan UNI Agency, Inc., Tokyo
English translation copyright © 2023 Takami Nieda

ISBN (paperback): 978-1-7398225-9-0
ISBN (ebook): 978-1-915829-00-9
A catalogue record for this book is available from the British Library.

Printed and bound in Paju, South Korea
Cover design by Bumpei Kii
Typeset by Honford Star

1 3 5 7 9 10 8 6 4 2

Contents

Finger Bone

THE YELLOW ROAD stretched far and beyond.

Where the road would lead, I could not say. Perhaps it would not deliver us to Salamaua. We had no choice but to press on.

I'd stopped walking some time ago. With my body propped against the base of a tree resembling a Japanese elm, I gazed at the husks of men shambling past. Hunched forward as if weighed down by a heavy burden, they dragged one foot, then the other, slowly across the yellow dirt, towing long shadows behind them. One shadow receded toward a pair of ankles, its owner listing forward. A thud. The human stirred no more. As the sun traced an arc across the sky, his shadow ticked around him like a sundial.

On my stomach rested a steel mass, which I gripped with both hands, as though it were my spirit. I thought of the finger bone tucked away in my rucksack. The one I'd stored in the bento box. I'd made a pinky promise with the bone.

Perhaps I should have died that night in the foxhole. Should have taken shrapnel in the belly and died. Perhaps it was because I'd failed to accomplish this, I realize now, that my fate became tied to the yellow road.

Pinned inside the foxhole, I had felt a searing heaviness in my left shoulder. I touched it, and something warm dribbled down my hand. The palm was caked with red mud. I took out a triangular bandage from my pack and wrapped the wound, starting at the armpit and over the shoulder several times. I bit down on one end of the bandage, held the other end with the right hand, and pulled with all my might. A whimper escaped my lips. A greasy sweat beaded my face. The searing heaviness gave way to the horrible cracking of bone. Waves of pain crested and ebbed in time with my heartbeat.

A grenade exploded nearby, raining red dirt, branches, and palm fronds around me. My schoolmate Furuya had died only moments ago. He lay on his side in the grass, half his head torn off. His blood streaked for several meters across the grass as if it'd been dashed by someone's hand. Am I going to die like Furuya? I hunkered down in the hole, cradling my rifle.

The noise of guns and artillery ceased before sundown. The mountainside of Isurava turned quiet, and I sensed the presence of death, sensed it creeping toward the foxhole where I lay crouched. Holding the helmet on my head with one hand, I ventured a look out from the lip.

Two shots rang in my ears. It wasn't me that was hit. I sighted Sergeant Tanabe slumped over the edge of his foxhole, clutching his bayoneted rifle. A red stain unfurled like a flower on the back of his uniform. Standing in the grass was an Australian soldier, his rifle aimed at the sergeant. He hadn't seen me yet. I gripped the bolt handle of my rifle and pulled it back. I maneuvered to bring the muzzle out of the hole. The barrel snagged in the dirt and a pathetic sound of metal rang out. My left arm shuddered in pain. The young, pale-faced soldier stood blankly, his blue eyes staring at my head poking out of the hole. I squeezed the trigger. The bullet bore into the base of his neck. He squawked something in English, and with a hand pressed against his neck spouting blood, he fell over backward. Dead. Black blood spread across the grass in the setting sun. After ascertaining his end, I dropped back into my hole.

Dusk seeped across the jungle depths on the island which was located south of the equator. The foxhole, barely large enough for one man, was being overtaken by darkness, until I could no longer make out my hand. The moon rose above the palm trees soon after. I glimpsed the stained bandage on my shoulder in the pale moonlight. The blood on my hands had hardened and turned the color of iron sand. The air smelled of blood and steel. Gangly roots peeked out from the earth about me. The hole was littered with spent cartridges, cigarette butts, withered palm fronds, clumps of red dirt.

I tried crawling out of the hole once or twice but couldn't summon the strength. I'd lost too much blood. I wasn't able to lift myself up with the good arm alone. I prayed for some friendlies to find me, but the Australians were just as likely to find me first. In the event of my discovery by the enemy, I was to take my life there in the foxhole. Gripped in my blood-caked hands was the grenade, which had been saved for exactly that purpose. A Type 99 hand grenade detonates four seconds after pulling the firing pin and striking the head of the fuse. When the time came, I would draw the steel cylinder toward me and ball myself up like a pill bug. Don't think about anything for four seconds. Imagine your warm belly being blown open and you're likely to throw your only grenade out of the hole. The foxhole was one I dug the night before. If you die here, that would mean you dug your own grave, I thought, and had to laugh. With the grenade snuggled against my belly, I drifted into a shallow sleep.

The next morning, I was awakened by a flood of sunshine. The dark-blue sky expanded above me. At times, a shadowy figure peered in, hindering my view, then moved off, and the sky opened up again. Voices from somewhere in the distance. Where did the grenade go? I couldn't move my body. I faded again.

Days later, I was sitting on a bed at a field hospital, rubbing the knob that had formed on the left side of my back. I felt something hard beneath the flesh and the bandage. A hardness not of bone, but of lead. It was to have the lead removed that I waited to see the doctor. That night in the foxhole, I had escaped being killed and from having to kill myself. A squad of friendlies had found me and pulled me out of the hole.

I wasn't taken to the field hospital directly but to a facility in a palm grove near Isurava. Whether it could properly be called a hospital was debatable as it was nothing more than a Type 95 canopy tent tied to some palm trees, some stretchers placed on the ground. Men with critical cases of malaria slept on the stretchers, in still silence, their faces the color of earthenware. Some of them might have been dead already. The Army doctor applied iodine on my wounds. "A couple of bullet wounds," he drawled. "Looks like they went clean through. You'll heal soon enough." Then he bandaged up the shoulder and gave me a shot to prevent tetanus and gangrene. The listless man with pouched eyes didn't look much like a doctor, perhaps due to his impotence. With supply lines stalled, quinine had become hard to come by. The patients on the stretchers were not being treated but were merely waiting for death to take them.

Unlike the tent hospital in the palm grove, the field hospital to where I was eventually transferred had a proper roof, a floor, and walls. Three rows of wooden beds, which appeared to have been built hastily on-site, were arranged down the length of the infirmary. Grass shades hung in the windows and outside was a modest veranda. That a hospital of this size could be built so far inland was impressive. There must have been a number of carpenters in the detachment assigned to build it. Sometime after coming to the hospital, I began to feel an odd sensation in the back of my shoulder. Whenever I turned over in bed, something cold and foreign rolled beneath the skin. Soon a small knob formed, and it grew larger by the day. The flesh was trying to push the lead out of my body. The doctor back at the palm grove had left a bullet inside me.

The doctor here stuck his head out of the examination room and called my name. I quit rubbing the knob and got up from the bed. A soldier on crutches missing a leg hobbled out of the examination room as I went in.

I sat down on the stool, and after I explained my condition, the doctor came around to my back. Before me was a table and beyond that a medicine cabinet. The shelves were lined with bottles of iodine tincture, Wilson's ointment, and bismuth subnitrate. Empty bottles of quinine were strewn in a pile in a corner of the room. The sunlight trickling in between the palm fronds cast an amber shadow behind the bottles. On the table was an aluminum tray containing several surgical instruments. The scalpel and forceps glinted coldly in the room which was otherwise lit softly by the sun. There was a time I met a soldier who got shot up in the thigh by a Curtis P-40 fighter. The bullet holes were tiny, as American machine guns are of a smaller caliber. The thigh was riddled with pits where the bullets had exited. Each wound had to be pried open with forceps to remove the bullets that had gotten lodged. It must have smarted pretty good when the bullets went into him and smarted pretty good when the forceps entered the slits and dug them out. The doctor took a look at the knob on my back and grunted. He stroked the hairs on his chin. He picked up a scalpel from the aluminum tray and drew the blade over the blue flame of the alcohol lamp. He grabbed hold of my shoulder from behind. I straightened my back.

"Hunch your back a bit, will you? To stretch the skin."

I bent forward slightly, steadying my eyes on the tips of

my lace-up boots. The doctor pinched the knob between two fingers, pulled the skin taut, and made an incision at the base. Sweat sheened my forehead. I gritted my molars to fight back the pain. The scalpel cut deeper. It couldn't have been more than a centimeter or two, yet the pain felt as if the entire length of the blade had slipped inside. The tip of the blade touched something fibrous, arresting my breathing. Something soft, warm, and rubbery. When the blade sliced into it, I felt the sure pain of cold steel. Suppressing the groan in the back of my throat, I expelled a deep breath and felt the warm blood running down my back. There was a metallic rattle behind me, and the doctor pressed a gauze pad against the wound. On the aluminum tray was a bloody slug about the size of a fingertip flecked with flesh.

After bandaging up the wound, the doctor stuck his head out of the examination room and called the name of the next patient. As I went out, a dark-complexioned soldier emaciated with malaria walked in, probably to get an injection of Ringer's solution.

The wound throbbed so sharply that I couldn't lie down. I sat on the edge of the bed and waited for the pain to settle. A young medic came around and starting at one end, called out to each of the patients in turn. The live ones let out a moan or a groan. The patient to my right let out neither. After checking the patient's pulse and pupils, the medic slid a ply-wood board beneath the deceased's hand. He took out a knife and brought the blade down on the soldier's finger as if he were cutting a carrot and moved on.

"That's a lucky man to have his finger taken for his family like that," the patient on my left muttered, propping himself up in the bed. "Die in the jungle all alone, and all the family gets back home is three stones."

The man's face was almost entirely covered in bandages.

The enormous island floats in the ocean, just south of the equator. The peninsula extends southeast from the island, like a bird's tail. Though it appears narrow on a map, the peninsula measures three hundred kilometers wide. Our objective, we were told, was to make landfall on the peninsula's eastern coast, cut through the jungle, and take the American base at Port Moresby on the western coast. "MacArthur himself is on that western base. The man who kills him will be immortalized in history," blustered an officer, but who knew if any of it was true. About midway into our advance, I was wounded near the village of Isurava and transported behind the lines. One time, Sergeant Tanabe had shown me a rough map, where beyond Isurava were names like Kagi, Nauro, and Ioribaiwa, written in pencil. None of us was in possession of an accurate map. No such map existed, as no one had ever attempted to cross the island on foot. We were to map the terrain as we went. Beyond Ioribaiwa, we were told, lay the western coast where the American base was situated.

The Japanese Army continued its advance down the length of the peninsula according to plan. According to plan, at least, until I was wounded at Isurava. Despite being slowed by a number of skirmishes, within days, the Army expanded its territory to the center of the peninsula. Food was scarce, but once we captured the western base, we would be able to secure a food supply. Strike swiftly and procure supplies locally—that had been the Army's strategy before, and so it was on the island. There was, however, something unsettling about the way the enemy engaged us. Every time the Japanese Army took the fight to the American and Australian forces, they retreated without putting up much of a fight. When the Japanese forces chased them down to make another attack, they retreated again.

"A disappointment, really," one officer scoffed. "The white man is not a soldier but a tourist."

Indeed, that was one way of looking at it.

The field hospital stood nestled against the mountains. No doubt the Army had chosen the site fearing discovery by the enemy. Past the veranda was a makeshift courtyard

Finger Bone

dotted with tree stumps, and beyond that loomed the jungle. Backed by the mountains and fronted by the jungle, the courtyard was completely enclosed save the hill in the western corner. The gentle slope was carpeted with undergrowth and flowers swaying in the breeze. Every day, the sun peeked out from over the mountains and dipped behind the hill. It was how I determined due west.

The words "XX Division Field Hospital No. 3" had been carved with a knife on a tree at the entrance.

In the afternoons, a group of wounded soldiers exercised in the courtyard. They moved about slowly, stretching, bending, reaching. Lying in a hospital bed for days on end weakened the legs. When we went back to the front, we would have to resume the march. If you fell behind and got ambushed, you were going to get killed. I stretched like the others and took a stroll around the courtyard afterward. The landscape was verdant with vegetation. Plants with thick, droopy leaves. Oversized flower petals of red and yellow, mottled with black. Patches of bright colors like those found on a paint palette. In one corner stood a tree thrusting its branches toward the sky. Beneath it was a bench, placed there perhaps as a lark by the detachment put in charge of building the hospital. There sat a soldier taking a rest.

"Care for a smoke, friend?"

It was the soldier whose face was wrapped in bandages. The end of his cigarette glowed red in the tree's heavy shadow. His mouth was covered, making it appear as though the cigarette was being smoked through the dressing. I sat on the bench next to him and took a cigarette from the proffered pack. After putting the cigarette in my mouth, I looked down at my arm in the sling and realized I couldn't strike a match. Noticing my predicament, the man lit another cigarette, took a pull on it, and held it out in my direction. The first drag in weeks made my head spin. The last time I'd smoked was the night in the foxhole.

"It tastes strange."

"I bought it at the canteen in Kokopo. It's an acquired taste."

The man named Sanada was a private and twenty-one, like me. When they'd made land at Buna, rather than commence the march inland, his unit was tasked with building roads at Giruwa.

"I'm no engineer. Never figured I'd be humping a pickaxe on a construction job."

Sanada tilted his chin and blew out a stream of smoke.

"After a couple of weeks, we got our marching orders inland. Loaded up with plenty of food supplies. I guess supplies to the frontline have been lagging. We got ambushed by some guerillas in the jungle, and *this* is my honorable wound in battle."

Finger Bone

He pointed at his right eye hidden in the gauze.

Several soldiers continued to stretch in the courtyard. Gingerly, mindful of their wounds. Slowly, like old folks lazing in the sun.

Watching the orange embers creeping up his cigarette, Sanada said, "There's only so many cigarettes a man can smoke while he's alive."

He tossed the stubby remains on the ground.

Patients died at the hospital daily. Many died of malaria. They mostly experienced the same symptoms: three to four days of high fever, followed by a period of recovery. Just when they thought they'd come through the worst of it, they were stricken with fever again. After a third cycle of this, half of the patients died. After the fourth, another half. Like the tent hospital in the palm grove, the field hospital had run out of quinine and acrinamine long ago.

After repeated bouts of fever, some patients became delirious. One malaria patient, who'd been tossing and turning with night sweats, jumped out of bed and pattered to and fro taking orders for soba noodles. The wounded soldiers shouted their orders in turn. Kitsune soba! Tanuki soba! Tempura soba! Put extra tempura crisps in mine! The voices rang across the infirmary, and suddenly, the field hospital in the South Pacific was a soba shop along the Sumida River. The shopkeeper, spotting a medic returning from tending to the dead, called out, "Welcome!"

"The place looks busy," replied the medic.

The shopkeeper turned to his empty bed, growling, "Hey, don't just sit there. Bring the man some water." Hearing this, all the rest of us could do was look down. Pushing aside the grass shade hung at the entrance of the infirmary like a noren curtain, the shopkeeper brought a hand to his forehead, narrowed his eyes, and looked somewhere distant. I couldn't tell what he was looking at from my bed. After a while, he shuffled back to the "kitchen" and died not long after.

Another time, back at the garrison in Buna, a medic had gotten so overwhelmed with malaria patients he cried out, "Mosquitoes are the Devil's vermin!" The place was swarming with mosquitoes, and you could not sleep until you squashed every last one that got through the net lest you risk malaria. There wasn't a mosquito in sight at the field hospital, though, perhaps because there weren't any ponds or marshes in the vicinity. Or, maybe the elevation was higher than I was aware. "You seen the bats flying around at dusk? You don't see any mosquitoes because the bats eat up all the larvae," one patient explained, but who knew if it was true. Not once did I see a patient contract malaria at the hospital. They either

Finger Bone

came with symptoms already or became infected somewhere else and got sick at the hospital after a period of dormancy.

The empty beds grew conspicuous. At some point, the sick and wounded had stopped arriving. Perhaps the Japanese forces had taken control of the US base on the western coast. Once the base hospital was built, the sick and wounded would no longer have to be transported behind the lines. Patients died daily, and the empty beds became more numerous with every passing day. Vacant beds dressed with white sheets soaked up the sun. The sheets were the picture of cleanliness, despite the death that transpired there.

Whenever a patient died, one of the medics came around to cut off a finger. They'd cut off so many that they had gotten good at it. They placed the blade at the joint and put their full weight upon the back of the knife. Watching them making short work of their task, I thought them cold, as they'd become inured to death.

There was hardly any blood when the finger was taken. Only a small quantity dribbled onto the cutting board. I asked a medic about it out of curiosity.

"The pump's already stopped working," he replied. "It's only what's left in the blood vessels that drips out.

When I thought about it, it made perfect sense.

"We really shouldn't … cut off the finger of a patient who

might have died of infection. But we're careful not to leave any residue. Circumstances being what they are, the discretion is ours."

Some days passed since I was brought to the hospital, and a new layer of skin began to form over the wounds in my shoulder. The pain and swelling, though, were slow to subside. The doctor examined me, holding my elbow and straightening my arm to the side. A leaden pain ran up my arm, and I muffled a gasp.

"Hurts, does it?"

I contorted my face and nodded, and nodded again.

The doctor undid the bandages, picked up a dressing pad with forceps, and soaked it in solution. He cleaned each of the three bullet wounds with the dressing, colored red with iodine. Then he examined the incision where the knob used to be and applied iodine to it.

"The bullet might have fractured the bone upon entry. We'll put a splint on the arm. Try not to move it for a while."

Once the splint was in place, I could barely move my left arm, only slightly left and right.

The Army doctor wore a beard. He had a habit of stroking it whenever he fell into thought. During one examination, I came to learn he used to work at a sanatorium in Kamakura

Finger Bone

before he was called into service. "It sits on a hill overlooking Shichirigahama Beach, a nice facility with an even better view," said the doctor. "Plenty of sun, a pleasant breeze coming in from the sea. On a sunny day, you can see Sagami Bay clear to the horizon."

The doctor stared out the window awhile, stroking his chin, one cheek painted by the sun. The hill sloping into the foothills was visible from the examination room. Patches of flowers resembling balsam were in bloom. They spread their red petals with single determination, bathing in light. "There was a girl with spinal tuberculosis," the doctor continued.

"She took a liking to me. But she was very sick, so it was very hard. I find myself thinking of her often since I arrived here. I hope she can hold on until I can go back and see her. It would be about two now in Shichirigahama. About time for open-air therapy."

Open-air therapy entailed beds being arranged in the sanatorium's courtyard, so patients could convalesce in the fresh air. Perhaps the girl was staring at the inside of her eyelids turned translucent in the sun, thinking of the doctor who was called away to war.

The bed to my right remained vacant. The one beyond that was occupied by a private named Shimizu. He was usually hunched over cross-legged on his bed, drawing. He sketched quick, sure lines across the straw paper with a pencil. Sometimes he sketched what he could see from the infirmary. Other times, he sketched things he couldn't. Cherry blossom trees alongside food stalls, a shrine and a napping cat, a bicycle-drawn cart on a farm road—these he drew from memory.

One sketch depicting a riverside scene was a thing of beauty. Lines of willow trees stood along the cobblestoned streets flanking either side of the river. Their drooping tassels swayed gently in the wind. The leaves were drawn with gradually thinning lines to make them appear so. Along the tree-lined streets sat quaint houses with tiled roofs. One house was running a business of some kind. It appeared to be a tofu shop. Beneath a noren curtain, a man in a white cap was dipping a wooden paddle into a tank of water. A customer held out a bowl and waited for his tofu. None of the buildings were taller than the willow trees, so as to make the sky appear bigger.

"That's really something the way you're able to draw from imagination. Do you memorize scenes, like a snapshot or something?"

Shimizu thought about it for a moment. "I wouldn't say memorize exactly. It's just that I've been drawing ever since I can remember. I don't know how to explain it myself. Besides, this scene is one I've known since I was a kid."

Finger Bone

"It's impressive just the same. Especially since I have no aptitude for drawing."

Shimizu scratched his head bashfully with the bandaged nub of his left arm. He'd taken shrapnel from a grenade and his left arm was rounded into a stump at the wrist. He'd also contracted malaria, but his symptoms had subsided.

One day, Shimizu stopped drawing. When I asked why, he said he had no more pencils. I'd brought some Yacht military-use pencils, so I offered him a couple. Shimizu cried that I was a life saver and gave me a tin of Shiseido tooth powder in return. And so, with a brand-new pencil, he took up drawing again. One line and another extended and overlapped in blank space, giving shape to an image.

"I suppose the joints in your hand, the nerves in your fingers remember exactly how the lines should be drawn. It isn't something that can be learned in a day. It's really something."

Shimizu chuckled. "I'm naturally left-handed. I only started drawing with my right hand after I got here."

Life with an arm in a sling was an inconvenience at first. But after a couple days, I got used to it. I wasn't able to hold my mess tin and the lid at the same time. After getting some soup ladled into the tin, I went back to my bed, set the soup down, and went back with the lid to get some rice. To take a drink from my canteen, I removed the cap by clamping the bottle between my feet. To sharpen a pencil with a knife, I placed the pencil between the bed and my foot with the sharp end sticking out from the edge, and I hunched over like I would to clip my toe nails. With repetition, I no longer thought these tasks to be a burden. They felt as though they were things I'd done all my life.

There was one thing I could not do with one hand alone.

One night after dinner, the residents of the infirmary staged an informal talent show. A private who used to be a singer in a jazz band performed a tune a cappella. Everyone froze for an instant upon hearing the opening strains of what might be considered the enemy's music, but there weren't any officers in the audience to notice. The singer began to snap his fingers and sway in time to the music. His droll manner got the rest of us swinging, too. After hitting the last note, he bowed, and the room exploded into applause. While the others cheered, I stared down in silence. I'd made to clap, but my one free hand whiffed the air.

About two weeks after I arrived at the hospital, Sanada and I were maintaining our rifles beneath a tree, shaded from the afternoon sun. We took our time wiping down the barrel and muzzle with an anti-corrosion agent. Sanada asked to see my ammo. The muzzle of the Type 99 rifle measured 7.7 mm in diameter. I took out a five-round clip from my ammo bag and clapped it in his hand.

"Does the larger caliber give you more recoil?"

"Compared to the Type 38?" I nodded in the affirmative. "Fire off ten or so rounds and you get used to it."

Sanada brought the clip up to eye level and examined it. I opened the canister of leather oil and applied it to a rag. I worked the opaque liquid into the leather rifle sling, the cloying smell wafting in the air.

Afterward we went foraging for fruit. I had tasted mango and papaya at the garrison in Buna and found them sweet and good. If we could find one tree, we would have enough to last us a while. Sanada turned to me at the jungle entrance and asked if my rifle was loaded.

"This one soldier in the Philippines got eaten alive by a tiger in the jungle."

The sun was shut out from the jungle depths. Tall trees probably in the palm family covered the sky, while thick shrubs overlapped their branches beneath. Dense layers of green lidded over us. A bird, perhaps sensing our presence, hooted and flew off. Giant plants resembling butterbur sprouted from the ground. The shoots were as thick as human arms and their leaves large enough to hide behind. The glossy leaves were plump as if they were filled with gelatin. Sanada called them "monster butterbur." The tropical climate seemed to turn the vegetation crude and unruly.

Once we were past the shrubs, the jungle opened up. Vines grew wild on the jungle floor, the leaf veins painted red. I thought they might be sweet potatoes. I pulled on the vines, and sure enough, purple potatoes came out of the earth. Sanada picked one up and shook his head.

"Poisonous. Seen plenty of these in Giruwa. Eat one, and you'll go into convulsions."

I dropped the potatoes on the ground. Perhaps finding a mango tree would not be so easily accomplished.

Sanada was still clutching the potato, motionless. Something was wrong. He was staring into the dark of the jungle. I traced his eyeline to find a man in the shadows. A black man. He was naked save the palm fronds around his torso. His white teeth and pink gums gleamed in the middle of his face. I snatched my rifle and made to point it at him, but Sanada put out a hand to stop me. We said nothing, and the black man said nothing. "*Apinun*," said Sanada, breaking the silence.

"*Mi painam kai kai.*" Sanada repeated *kai kai* and put his hands on his stomach. The black man watched us, quiet. He then motioned for us to follow and disappeared into the jungle.

"You speak the Kanaka language?"

Finger Bone

"Some of the Kanakas I got to know in Giruwa taught me a few words. I'm not sure if he understood me. Let's go find out."

We started after him down the animal trail. Beads of sweat dotted the man's bulging back. I could not begin to imagine the power coiled inside those lithe muscles. I kept a grip on the rifle so as to be able to ready it quickly. I worried about my arm. When I extended it to steady the firearm, a heavy pain shot through my flesh.

About a kilometer or so down the trail, the trees dissipated and the sun rained down upon us. Shielding my forehead with an arm, I spotted the Kanaka village.

The village spread along the hillside, a row of nipa huts lining the gentle slope. Beneath the eaves stood a group of black men. Women, too. The women's torsos were wrapped in grass skirts, their chests bare. One woman was squeezing the milk from her breasts into an earthen bowl. I fixated on the white milk coming out of the black breasts. She set the bowl down on the ground, drawing several black pigs around it.

Our guide gestured for us to wait and walked off toward the village. Several children came running out while we waited. Unlike the muscular physique of the adults, the children's bellies and palms were soft and plump. Their eyes were

round and innocent. Sanada greeted the children, "*Apinun,*
apinun."

"If we act friendly, maybe they'll give us something to eat."

Soon the black men came out of the huts and gathered
around us. I clutched my rifle and looked at Sanada. His eyes
were nervous. In that one moment of hesitation, we were
completely surrounded. The children hid behind the adults.
We smiled, but none of the black men smiled back. Wiping
the sweat from his forehead, Sanada quipped, "Hot weather
we're having," in Japanese, and repeated, "*Apinun.*" A strange
smell issued from their bodies. A pungent smell of meat and
boiled medicine. One of the men had a machete that touched
the ground. The long, rusty blade glistened with some kind
of substance.

With his head facing forward, Sanada leaned toward me
and whispered, "My rifle's not loaded. If something goes
wrong, fire one off."

It was a hell of a thing to tell a man with an arm in a sling.
I cast a casual glance behind me and saw the Kanakas had
us completely surrounded. That was when I remembered the
stories about the savage headhunters in the jungle depths.

I was damned if I was going to get my head chopped off,
forcing a stilted smile, repeating *apinun,* without knowing
what in the hell it meant. I put a hand on the grip of my rifle.

Finger Bone

They'd likely never seen one before, so I figured a warning shot would give us the distraction necessary to escape.

An old man stepped forward. He wore a feather decoration in his long, white hair and a cowrie-shell necklace. A ringed staff like that of a monk's khakkhara in his hand. He regarded us and pronounced, "Heitai,* Nippon," to our great shock. Sanada and the old man exchanged some words. Sanada took out a notebook from his rucksack, tore out several pages, and handed them to the old man. The black men retreated to their huts and soon returned bearing taro.

"The elder here is the captain of the village," explained Sanada. "He's giving us taro in exchange for paper. Seems we aren't the only Japanese soldiers to come to the village."

Later, the captain and Sanada negotiated an arrangement. He asked Sanada to teach the younger men of the village some Japanese. Thus began an impromptu Japanese class in the clearing. The Kanaka men sat around Sanada on the grass. They watched him enunciate the Japanese words and recited them back to him. I sat on a log and looked on from afar. Until then, the Kanakas had only existed in my imagination. All I'd known of them was that they were savages living primitively in the jungle. Seeing them now repeating konnichiwa, arigato, sayonara after Sanada, I realized they were flesh and

* *heitai* – soldier

blood. Beneath their skin flowed warm, red blood. I watched them raise their voices full of feeling. Sanada, drawing pictures on the ground with a stick, pointed the stick at me and proclaimed, "Nippon, heitai, jyoto."* I felt my face burn under their gaze.

When class was concluded, the Kanakas went away, murmuring "Arigato, arigato." Sanada sat down next to me and took a swig from his canteen.

"You're awfully friendly with the Kanakas."

"Hello, thanks, goodbye—that's all you really need to get by. Don't tell any of the others ..." Sanada lowered his voice. "When I injured my eye, I spent some time with a white soldier in the jungle. He had medical supplies, but nothing to eat. I had something to eat, but no medical supplies. At first sight, we pointed our rifles at each other. Then, I said hello, and he said konnichiwa back. Actually, it sounded more like cock-a-doodle-doo. That's when we both realized we'd been saved."

Hearing this, I recalled the blue eyes of the soldier I'd sighted from my foxhole. The blue eyes of the soldier I'd killed.

"Konnichiwa, arigato, sayonara in the Kanaka language is *apinun, tenkyu, lukim yu.* The word for food is *kai kai.* So, if

* *jyoto* – first-class

Finger Bone

you're ever hungry, you say *apinun* with a smile, then hold your stomach and say, *kai kai*, with a sad face, and if you're lucky, a kindly Kanaka will give you something to eat."

The captain approached from the other end of the clearing, jabbing the ground with his staff. Without a word, he handed Sanada some white shells and retraced his steps from whence he came.

"Our earnings."

"What are we supposed to do with those?"

"They may be shells to us, but to the Kanakas, this is money."

Sanada called out to a woman with a basket on her head, "Hey, there!" He handed her the shells, for which she gave him two mangoes.

We sat on a grassy hill and ate the fruit. How long had it been since I'd eaten a mango? The ripe flesh melted on my tongue, the sweetness filling my nostrils. The Kanaka children chased after each other at the foot of the hill. They were playing color tag or shadow tag, I couldn't tell which, but they appeared to be chasing each other according to some rule. Black shadows lengthened and receded from their bare feet and wavered across the grass. At times, the wind delivered their innocent laughter up the hill to where we sat.

"They don't have a care in the world."

Sanada said nothing in reply. His eyes were fixed on the children, the half-eaten mango forgotten in his hand. He seemed to have his mind on something else. Upon sensing my gaze, he gobbled down the rest of the fruit. Still, he said nothing until finally, scratching his head, he muttered, "I got a kid back home."

His bashful demeanor made me smirk.

"Are you missing your wife and kid?"

"My wife died soon after she gave birth."

I gave him a heavy nod.

"How soon after?"

"I guess around the time the baby started walking. He would hang onto the edge of the low table like so …"

As much as I waited, the rest of the story did not come. I peered sideways at him, but the right side of his face was covered in bandages. Only his ear was visible. "Anyway, you know kids," and there he ended the conversation. I knew why he'd cut his story short. He didn't want to reveal that fatherly side of himself.

The sun was slanting west when we left the village. The Kanaka men saw us to the edge of the jungle and waved say-onara. The evening sky blazed behind them, the billowing clouds tinted red. Sanada and I double-timed down the jungle trail before the shadows overtook us.

Finger Bone

It was dinnertime when we returned to the hospital. We took our rice in the lid and sweet potato soup in the mess tin. Pickled mustard greens accompanied the rice. The patients at the hospital were provided with decent meals. The fare was considerably better than the stuff we got on the march. That was largely thanks to the vegetable field nearby. Still, patients died regardless of the nutrition they consumed. "Once the body weakens beyond a certain point, it can't take in nourishment anymore," explained the doctor. "The stomach and intestines are already dead, so the nutrients simply come out the other end."

Sanada sat on the edge of his bed and shoveled the rice into his mouth. He ate the mustard greens, then shoveled more rice into his mouth. Shimizu, in contrast, ate slowly, taking time to savor every morsel. He wasn't able to hold the mess tin and chopsticks at the same time. He laid a plywood board on the bed, set the mess tin on top of it, and ate, sitting on his knees on the floor. I couldn't hold my mess tin either. I sat cross-legged on the bed, balancing the lid on one knee, and brought my face close to the rice and scooped it into my mouth with a fork.

The infirmary was quiet at dinnertime, quiet because the moaning and snoring stopped. A peaceful repast taken for the purpose of surviving. I thought about the Kanakas. They might be eating about now. Steamed taro, whitefish wrapped in banana leaves, bowls of palm wine. Were the black men feasting in the clearing? Were they practicing the Japanese words Sanada had taught them?

"What do you think the Kanakas aim to do by learning Japanese anyway?" I asked Sanada.

He looked up from his meal, his jowls moving as he chewed. "The island will be under Japanese rule when the war's over. Maybe they're planning to give sightseeing tours."

"Sightseeing?"

"I'd expect a few tourists would want to visit after the war—for the experience of seeing humanity's last uncharted territory. There will be a need for locals that speak Japanese. That's when the Kanakas are going to turn a profit doing business with the Japanese. Not in shell money, in Imperial money."

It was an interesting idea. I had hardly given a thought to life after the war. Perhaps in twenty or thirty years' time, tourists will flock to the island. Then perhaps the Kanakas who learned Japanese from Sanada will turn a profit doing business with the Japanese.

"What's this about the Kanakas?" Shimizu turned toward us, still sitting on the floor. We told him about the village some distance away.

Finger Bone

"Hm, they always seemed frightening to me." Shimizu turned back toward the bed and chewed his food slowly.

With a blackout order in effect, it was lights out as soon as it became dark. Two medics came around with palm oil lamps and called out to the patients. When one of the patients did not moan a reply, they put him on a stretcher and carried him out. There was a hole halfway up the western hillside into which the dead bodies were tossed. I lay on my side, hugging my stomach warmed by the sweet potato soup, thinking about the cold bodies being tossed into the black pit, about the corpses of the Japanese soldiers gradually decomposing to bone in the jungle, thousands of kilometers from home.

*

We set sail from Japan and made land on the island by way of Guam and New Britain. The township of Rabaul on New Britain was under Japanese occupation. Along the coast stood barracks and officers' quarters, and a complement of Zero fighters was parked alongside the airstrip in an area cleared of palm trees. While stationed in Rabaul, I came to know a private named Ichimura. He was fond of plays, as I was. Before the war, I used to take trips to the Tsukiji Shogekijo Theatre to catch the latest Shingeki plays. Ichimura had graduated from Rikkyo University's English Department, and owing to his English proficiency, he was charged with looking after the prisoners of war. The POW camp was located in a meadow on the south end of the base, encircled by iron fencing. I'd run into Ichimura coming out of the camp, and he'd said in exasperation, "The Greater East Asia War is as good as won! The Americans aren't any kind of soldiers. I asked one of them why he didn't kill himself knowing he was going to get captured, and he answered he was afraid of suicide. You should have seen his big, puppy-dog eyes when he said it. His soul is withered to the core. He's nothing but a tourist on a camping trip with his buddies."

I'd never seen a POW camp up close before. I once watched a POW working in the field from afar. The American wearing a white threadbare shirt was cleaning the barrel of one of our mountain guns. Did he have puppy-dog eyes? I couldn't tell.

Ichimura ended up staying in Rabaul as a prison guard at the camp. We promised to see a play together after the war and parted ways. Then, the transport ship took me west across the South Seas.

The ship arrived off the coast of Buna on the eastern peninsula in the dead of night. It was a starless night. When the ship

Finger Bone

cut its engines, the surging waves echoed around us. On the far side of the beach stood the silhouettes of palm trees, a color darker than night, waving at us. The clammy breeze dampened my cheeks. I felt a stir I'd not felt in Guam or in New Britain. A stir signaling our arrival at the outer reaches of Imperial territory, the frontline where death was all but certain.

The sergeant at the Buna garrison distributed oval-shaped brass plates called ID tags. My ID number and unit designation were engraved on it in kanji numerals. He told us to bring him any letters we wanted sent by the end of the day. The combination of the ID tag and the letter seemed to portend something ominous. We listened to the sergeant bloviate about the action in Singapore and the Malay Peninsula. "The momentum was ours. We were unstoppable. Like boulders rolling down a hill. The British and Australians took one look at us and were tripping over themselves to escape. A sad sight, really."

I wrote a letter to my family. Ever since I watched the homeport disappear from aboard the transport ship, I tried not to think about them. I didn't want them in my head as I was about to kill the enemy. A half second's hesitation and I might be the one to get killed. That was why I'd decided to keep thoughts of family at bay. But seeing as I was addressing the letter to them, I wouldn't have been able to write anything if I didn't take time to reflect

When our deployment orders to the southern front were handed down, we were granted a three-day leave. I troubled over whether to visit home, but my schoolmate Fujiki had goaded me into going. "Maybe if you pray at your grandparents' altar, you'll get lucky." I arrived after sunset and stiffly slid open the door to the house. My father was in a foul mood and did not speak a word to me. He sat at the dining table, saying nothing, and wolfed down the red bean rice, which my mother had made to celebrate my return. Despite being the first-born son, I had moved out of the house, choosing a life of idleness in Kyobashi, Tokyo instead of succeeding the family farm. It was no wonder my father was upset by my visit. I was due back at the barracks the next morning, so it had been my father's only opportunity to express his displeasure. He certainly didn't have to eat a second time after I'd arrived, just so he could show how cross he was with me.

My mother, on the other hand, was in high spirits, warming a pot in the kitchen, humming a song. She placed the mackerel miso soup and perilla-wrapped eggplant on a tray and brought them to the table. She set the bowls and small dishes before my father and me. Feeling hemmed in, I wolfed down the red bean rice like my father. My younger sister Chizuru came next to me, saying, "Write me when you get there." She gave me a good-luck satchel to ward off bullets.

Finger Bone

The good-luck satchel turned out to be exactly that. When the doctor examined my bullet wounds, he'd said, "You got lucky." If any of the bullets had been a few centimeters lower, it might have damaged the heart valve and killed me instantly.

Perhaps Chizuru's good-luck satchel had repelled the bullets at the last moment.

My letter was flagged by censors, and I had to rewrite it three times. I don't know what happened to that letter. With any luck, it should have arrived in Japan by now. If not, it was likely at the bottom of the Bismarck Sea.

En route to Buna, I took the occasion to look out at the Solomon Sea for a good while. Though I did not know the exact route the transport ship had taken, since New Ireland was to our east when we hit the open sea, that would have put us in the Solomon Sea and not the Bismarck Sea. Fujiki and Furuya were alive then. One day, Fujiki and I went on lookout duty on the crow's nest. The watchtower was affixed to the mast about a dozen meters' climb up the rope ladder. We stood back-to-back, Fujiki watching the starboard side, while I watched portside. We lit up our cigarettes, without the worry of any senior officers finding out. Though we'd heard transport vessels had gone down in these parts, the ocean that day was peaceful. Not a friendly, enemy fighter or vessel in sight.

"Strange, isn't it?" muttered Fujiki, his back against mine. "Bumping into each other at the medical examination at the conscript office and ending up together on the South Seas beyond the equator like this? Even Furuya wound up in our unit. Some coincidence."

"I hear it was intentional," I answered. "The units were formed with men from the same region to strengthen unity."

The ocean was a mix of deep greens and blues. The water's surface reflected the sunlight and sparkled like stained glass. I imagined schools of tropical fish swimming beneath the surface. The shallows carpeted with coral. Not a sign that an American submarine packing torpedoes might be cruising below. At the farthest point where the sparkling ocean ended, the horizon stretched from end to end. A thin line for the purpose of delineating the ocean from the sky. The line was curved slightly, proving the ship was floating on the surface of the Earth.

Fujiki tapped my shoulder. When I turned around, the cigarette in my mouth fell at my feet. White caps spiked the water on the starboard side behind us. The waves looked too odd to be the wakes of torpedoes. In fact, the waves were streaking in a straight line away from the ship.

Fujiki lowered his binoculars and murmured, "Dolphins."

It was a pod of dolphins spooked by the ship's engine noise.

"I don't want to die before we reach Buna," said Fujiki,

Finger Bone

lighting up another cigarette. "We're not sailors. I'll be damned if a torpedo gets us."

Looking out at the ocean, Fujiki began to warble a sentimental song called, "Blues for Farewell," famously recorded by Noriko Awaya. "Noriko-san's voice has a curious resonance," said Fujiki. "The way her voice trembles on the high notes sounds like yellow butterflies fluttering around white clovers." Fujiki's singing was drowned out by the wind. But since we were standing back-to-back, the reverberations struck me directly. For some reason, I was reminded of elementary school. Of being bested by Fujiki at everything, of thinking of Fujiki as a rival before realizing I couldn't compete, of telling myself he was special and that he was born on another planet to assuage a child's—my own—fragile heart. I remembered going to the barracks one time to watch Fujiki get slapped by a veteran soldier. I suppose it was my way of getting revenge.

Fujiki returned with one cheek swollen and noticed me watching. "Hell, I forgot to bite down. Now my mouth's bleeding," he mumbled, rinsing his mouth at the watering area outside. It was a sunny day in winter. He swished the water in his mouth, his cheeks puffed out, staring at me all the while. It was then I forgot my petty jealousy. That was when I knew he was special.

"They're not going to get you," I said.

Fujiki went on crooning for a while, then turned to me. "You know the difference between getting shot and not getting shot? Dumb luck."

"They're not going to get you," I repeated, as much as to convince myself that I'd pull through the war. Fujiki wasn't going to die because he was special, I told myself, and I wasn't going to die because I was in the same unit as him.

We came under fire from behind at Isurava. We took cover and readied to return fire, but Sergeant Tanabe waved us off. The shooters in the trees were friendlies. Skirmishes had broken out everywhere, and the foothills were in chaos. The friendlies had seen us on the move and mistaken us for Australian forces. The shooting ceased almost immediately. Everyone got up, some of them grumbling their relief. I got to my feet and swatted away the dry grass from my uniform. One soldier did not get up. It was Fujiki. He'd taken a bullet in the head and died instantly.

His death nearly broke me. It was probably the same for Furuya. The one man we'd believed wouldn't die was gone in a blink of an eye. A medic cut off his finger and put it in his service sack along with a lock of his hair. Furuya and I carried his body to a stream. Furuya held his legs, while I had him by the arms. I immediately understood why Furuya had

Finger Bone

grabbed hold of the legs first. There were rocks of different sizes all around the stream requiring you to look down as you walked, and if you were holding Fujiki's arms, you had to look directly down at this face.

The bullet had entered his left temple but had not come out. The slug was lodged in the skull. One of the medics had brushed a hand over Fujiki's eyes repeatedly to try to close them. The left eye protruded from the socket due to the impact of the bullet, so it would not shut. The medic had wrapped a cloth around his thumb and brought his weight down upon the eye to jam it back in. That was how his eye was closed.

That same eye was now open again a mere arm's length away from my face. His arms were still warm, his muscles soft, yet I could not detect any life in his brown, dilated eye. The eye had ceased to be a part of a life form; instead, it was an object.

We had intended to dig a grave near the stream, but it was not to be. Shots and explosions rang out, signaling an engagement. Dropping the corpse at our feet, Furuya and I took cover in the bushes. We cast a glance at Fujiki's body by the stream and clawed up the hill with our rifles.

That Furuya was an awful soldier. One time our transport vessel came under attack off the coast of New Ireland. We sighted the shadows of Lockheed bombers in the west, roaring toward us. We took up our rifles and waited for them on the deck. A rifle wasn't going to do us any good, but the first taste of the enemy had all of us excited.

"Those Lockheed bombers are gonna drop their bombs as soon as they're over us. This ship will sink like a sack of bricks," one man said, gawking at the sky. Hearing this, Furuya blanched in terror and began to shake uncontrollably.

"We'll be all right. You wait, our fighters are taking off from Rabaul right now." I patted Furuya on the back and smiled.

One after the next, friendly fighters shriveled up like matchsticks and fell out of the sky. The Lockheeds came roaring above us and dropped a swarm of small bombs. The pilots proved to not be very skilled. The water exploded around us, merely showering us in the aftermath.

Furuya was always shaking, even after we'd made land on the island. One misty morning, we came upon a gigantic tree known as an octopus tree. It appeared to be hundreds of smaller trees bundled together, which seemed like a smaller jungle sprawling inside the jungle. Our unit stood in a line, looking up at the haze of branches above us. Furuya stared with his mouth agape next to me, mumbling nonsensically, "What is this world?" He began to tremble. I sensed the presence of something inhuman beyond the mist. It might have been a mountain god like my grandmother used to speak of.

Finger Bone

Another time, Furuya and I were standing guard on a watchtower along the coast. It was around dawn on a frigid day for the South Seas. We leaned against the crossbars of the tower and kept our eyes peeled at the moonless ocean for enemy ships. For a while, we talked about home, military life, and other things until the conversation between us died. Perhaps it was the purple ocean and sky that held us in silence. Shaking off my idleness, I went back to searching for enemy ships. And then, the thin, white scar on Furuya's shaved head caught my eye. Since our deployment, I slipped into an indescribable mood every time I glimpsed it.

Furuya's family ran a bathhouse called the Matsu no Yu. When we were in elementary school together, Furuya had offered to give his friends discounts, so a few of us went for a soak. Furuya had been uncharacteristically excitable that day, and he slipped, hit his head on the tile, and passed out. The soapsuds on the tiled floor turned pink. When he returned from the hospital with four stitches, his old man yelled, "Are you stupid? The son of a bathhouse keeper falling in the bath and getting taken to the hospital!" Furuya had been close to tears.

Taking my eyes off his scar, I pulled out a Homare-brand cigarette from my breast pocket. As I brought a match up to light it, Furuya turned from gazing at the horizon and looked squarely at me. "I'm scared of dying," he said. Amidst all the others preparing to fight bravely to their deaths, he was so straight in his declaration that I spat out my cigarette. The cigarette fell toward the beach, leaving a trail of embers. A tiny spark flared in the purple dark below.

Staring at the ocean blending into the dawning sky, he continued, "I thought about why I'm scared of dying. It's because we don't know what happens when we do."

It was a childish thought but it was just like Furuya. He said nothing more after that. He seemed to be listening to the waves. I couldn't bring myself to say anything to him.

What Furuya had been trying to do when he died, I do not know. Nor will I ever. I had been standing in my foxhole, my elbows propped on the lip, returning fire against the Australian attack. A soldier darted past me from behind. It was Furuya. He'd run out of his foxhole into the crossfire, trying to reach another foxhole. He was cradling something in his arms. I was so taken by the sight of him that I stopped shooting. From the break in the dust clouds, I discerned he was holding an ammo box but couldn't tell what he was trying to do. In the next instant, I saw a purple flash and was slammed against the wall of the foxhole. I saw Furuya dead, his head cracked open by shrapnel.

I might have shouted his name. Before I knew it, I was

Finger Bone

crawling out of the foxhole to try to reach him. But my left shoulder was pulled down by a powerful force. Don't go, it seemed to say. I fell back into my hole. A short time later, I felt a searing heaviness in my left shoulder. I touched it, and my hand came away dripping with blood.

*

After the pain of my wounds subsided, I went to work in the field with some of the others.

About a kilometer's walk from the hospital, there was a fan-shaped field where sweet potatoes, corn, mustard greens, and azuki beans were being cultivated. The area had been cleared by the same detachment that built the hospital. The seeds they'd sown had sprouted and the crops had grown enough to be eaten. Tassels drooped on many of the corn stalks. The azuki beans, before they podded, were beginning to bear yellow flowers. It was strange to see seeds that had been brought over from Japan taking root in a foreign land, bearing fruit and grain.

When we'd finished harvesting what we needed and were preparing to head back to the hospital, one soldier stopped and stared at the eastern sky. Moments later, the ground rumbled beneath our feet. We dropped the corn we'd harvested and took cover in the trees. The tree trunks quaked, suggesting the planes were flying low. We could not sight them. Only their roar was heard bearing down on us.

The corn nestled in Shimizu's good arm fell to the ground.

We watched the steel bellies of the twin-fuselage Lockheeds rumble across our fan-shaped view of the sky.

When the work in the field was done, Sanada, Shimizu, and I ventured down to the creek.

The creek was at the bottom of a steep hill which sloped down from behind the vegetable field. There was a small waterfall slightly upstream, a gentle babble echoing about. Rocks of various sizes, some as big as humans, lay all along the creek. Sago palms drooped their fleshy leaves on the slope on the other side. Flowers resembling wild chrysanthemums bloomed on the higher portions of the slope which seemed to get plenty of sunlight.

I crouched at the water's edge and dipped my hand in. A bone-piercing chill crept up my wrist to my elbow. Like the ocean I'd seen from the transport ship, the water sparkled like emeralds. Beneath that sparkling surface were stones and moss-covered branches. Sun streaks drifted over my submerged hand, shifting and changing shape.

Sanada walked unsteadily along a fallen tree lying across

the creek. When he reached the end, he got down on his haunches and took a drink of water.

Shimizu was sitting on a flat rock, gazing at the flowers on the slope. He seemed to be committing the scene to memory, so he could sketch it later.

We kept quiet and listened to the murmurs of the creek. I felt a residual tingling in my eardrum caused by the roar of the Lockheed planes earlier. It was the first time I'd seen that many enemy aircraft since I arrived on the island.

About three weeks after I was admitted to the hospital, a messenger turned up and delivered a letter to the doctor. The messenger with slivered eyes took a drink of water from the bucket and disappeared into the dark jungle. After shutting himself away in the examination room for half an hour, the doctor went out to the courtyard for a stretch. He sat down on a tree stump and lit a cigarette. He proceeded to smoke three of his precious cigarettes he only smoked on special occasions. I gathered the letter had not contained good news. Transfer orders to the newly-built base on the west coast were imminent. However, the doctor revealed nothing about the contents of the letter. About then, I realized the tingling swelled and waned to the hum of the creek.

"Do you want some corned beef?" Sanada asked from his perch on the edge of the fallen tree.

"Where are we going to find corned beef?"

Sanada walked back across the tree onto the bank and pulled out a can of corned beef from his rucksack.

"Where did you get that?"

"On our way to Isurava, we found some food cans that were probably air-dropped for remnant soldiers. We also found biscuits and cheese. The enemy's stuffing themselves with calories."

We sat on the bank and divided the can amongst ourselves. The over-salted meat slid into our stomachs, stimulating our senses. "I can feel the brain juices," I said, and Shimizu answered, "Me too." Sitting side-by-side as we were, it was plain to see the injuries we'd sustained. Sanada's face was in bandages, Shimizu's left wrist was in bandages, and my left arm was in a sling. To the enemy, we might have looked like a group of defeated soldiers drowning our sorrows in a can of corned beef.

When we polished off the can, we were quiet again. The can lay empty on the bank. The residual tingling in my eardrums faded into the murmurs of the creek.

"What do you say we get cleaned up!" Sanada said out of the blue and began stripping off his uniform until he was down to his breech cloth.

So, we decided to do a bit of laundry. Shimizu had a tin of

soap, so we were able to give our clothes a proper scrub with pumice stones. Afterward we laid them flat on the rocks.

While we waited for the clothes to dry, we skipped stones in our breech cloths. We competed to see how many times we could make a stone bounce across the water. I was hell at skipping stones. I could make a stone skim a good distance across the water, at times, clear to the other side. Shimizu, unable to use his throwing hand, was at a disadvantage. His stones bounced two or three times and sank.

"Ha! You call yourself a soldier in the Imperial Army!" Sanada chided, and Shimizu scratched his head.

We put on our parched clothes and left the creek behind.

Making our way back up the hill, we heard insects singing overhead. Their song gradually overtook the hum of the creek. I felt a pleasant fatigue of a kind I used to feel walking back from swimming in the local river as a kid, perhaps because I'd not exercised in a while. The soft uniform on my skin intensified that feeling. When we reached the top of the hill, the sun-drenched field was filled with insect song: a low, sustained cry like that of grasshoppers and intermittent ringing like that of crickets. Their song converged, creating a mighty chorus. The chirring insects were different from those found in Japan. Listening, as I gazed at the corn field bathed in the westering sun and at the azuki bean field swaying in the evening breeze, I imagined myself back in the homeland. A dragonfly sat on the end of a corn tassel. Or perhaps an insect like a dragonfly. Crooking its head toward the sunset, it slanted its transparent wings downward.

We returned to the hospital to find the doctor outside beneath the eaves. He was pickling mustard greens. He arranged the greens in the bottom of the barrel, covered them with plywood, and set a heavy rock on top as a weight. That was how we learned the mustard greens that frequently appeared in our meals were pickled by the doctor. Noticing me watching him, the doctor muttered, "Thank goodness my mother taught me how." He wiped a sleeve across his sweaty brows, his hands wet with juices, and glanced at the western hill, mumbling almost to himself, "I almost forgot, today is my birthday."

"How old are you turning, doctor?"

"Twenty-four. It's been a surprisingly long life."

"Are you married, sir?"

"I can't say that I've had luck with that. I thought about arranging a marriage, but I got called before I could."

"Are you sweet on that girl at the sanatorium? The one you treated for spinal tuberculosis?"

"Don't be silly. The girl is sixteen. I'm a doctor, she's a patient." The doctor's ears were red.

Finger Bone

I thought to give the doctor something in appreciation for his care and asked Shimizu to draw me something. He made me a drawing titled *Army Doctor Thinking*. It was a sketch of the doctor sitting in the examination room, his chin resting on the fingers of his right hand.

Accepting the gift, the doctor said, "It captures my features well. So much so, in fact, I don't think I'll be able to throw it away. Perhaps I'll hang it in the game room at the sanatorium," and smiled.

It rained for several days after that.

The rain, along with the labored breathing of the wounded, the moans of the fevered patients, echoed throughout the infirmary. Shimizu made a drawing titled *Field Hospital in the Rain*. It was a pencil sketch of the hospital in the rainy jungle seen from a distance. The way the raindrops misted over the building was rendered using the side of the pencil. He also rubbed a piece of gauze over the paper to create the effect of shadows.

"Strange how you're able to draw the hospital from the outside even as you're inside it." Sanada stated an opinion similar to one I'd given sometime before.

One soldier on crutches said, "This one's a beauty. Why don't we put it up somewhere?" And so, the finished drawings were put up on the walls with thumbtacks. Drawings titled *A Soldier Eating, A Soldier Exercising, Soldier with Gunnysack, Dendrobium and Swallowtail Butterfly, Corn Field on Southern Island, Palm Trees and the Solomon Sea* decorated the walls, turning the infirmary into something of an art gallery.

As the rain persisted, the increase in deaths became conspicuous. The doctor stroked his beard incessantly. Medical supplies were limited, so in many cases, his hands were tied. You would expect the doctor to have learned to divorce himself from his feelings. Unable to divorce himself completely, however, he took to stroking his chin.

"I assumed the best thing for a fever patient would be bed rest, but it seems doing nothing isn't quite the same as resting."

Lying in bed, I tried to think of things to help pass the tedium of a rainy day, but nothing came to mind. The longer I stared at the palmwood ceiling, listening to the rain, the more the walls seemed to close in on me. It wasn't that you couldn't go outside, just that you would get wet if you did. Venturing outside became a bother. Perhaps all the patients who'd died during that rainy period had simply died because they found being laid up with fever to be a bother. I turned to Sanada in the next bed.

"Anything we can do to pass the time during this spell we're having?"

Finger Bone

"There's always sleep."

"The doctor's troubled about all the patients he's been los-ing lately."

"How about a game of shogi?"

"Where are we going to get a shogi board?"

"We just need to make one."

Indeed, perhaps it was possible to fashion a board from the things in the infirmary. I thought about asking Shimizu to part with some of his paper, so we could make a board and the necessary shogi pieces, but Sanada balked at the idea.

"Look, it isn't shogi without the feel of the pentagonal wooden pieces in your hand. It isn't shogi without the sound of the pieces smacking against the wooden board. No, I re-fuse to play with paper."

With that, Sanada went outside and lugged back a tree stump he'd dug up. He left it to dry overnight, then drew a nine-by-nine grid on the surface. The shogi pieces were cut from the hacked off bits of the stump. The task of making the pieces was undertaken by a soldier who made Tsugaru kokeshi dolls back home. It was strange to contemplate a kokeshi maker humping a rifle on the frontline. "I'd-a done better work if I had a chisel …" He seemed dissatisfied by the end product, but the pieces were more than adequate.

For a time, shogi was all the rage in the infirmary. There

was one senior private who was exceptionally skilled. I had an opportunity to play him on one occasion. Gauging my abilities, he allowed me to take his rooks early. He allowed me, that is, so he could take advantage of his pawns. Though I'd believed myself to be at an advantage with my two rooks, he used his pawns and silver general to capture my pieces, and I could only watch dumbly as he went on the attack and put me in checkmate.

"You are a magician," said Sanada in awe.

"A shogi game without your pawns is a losing battle," said the senior private, with a hint of pride and sadness.

I also played Sanada on several occasions. Given how particular he'd been about the construction of the board and pieces, I assumed him to be a skilled player, but Sanada wasn't much of a player at all. His attacks were too rash. I let him capture some pieces to make the game more competitive. That very nearly was my downfall. We became deadlocked in a tight game, until I barely managed to wrest a victory away from him. With his arms folded across his chest, the senior private opined, "A fascinating game." He'd probably been aware that I had taken it easy on Sanada and that Sanada knew it, too.

One afternoon, Sanada, Shimizu, the senior private, and I were deep in a game of yamakuzushi. We took turns sliding the shogi pieces away from the pile in the middle of the board, trying to do so without any of the pieces making a hitting sound, as was the goal of the game. We had our ears pricked so we could catch any sounds the other players made in attempting to remove a piece. At the time, a curious rumor was going around the infirmary. It was that Guadalcanal was Heaven on Earth—

After they chased the Americans off the island, our boys have been feasting on deep-fried tofu and rice, eating hard-tack slathered with butter, drinking taro shochu, and holding sumo contests.

Given that no one here seemed to know the coordinates of the frontline on the island, much less the South Sea region, there was no telling where such a rumor had originated. Thinking back to my time at the base on Rabaul, I thought the rumor about Guadalcanal plausible. "I wish I'd gotten on a boat to Heaven," grumbled a soldier who'd come down with fever for a third time. He continued, "Heaven ... ah, Heaven ..." while we quietly slid the shogi pieces away from the pile. Suddenly, the same soldier let out a cry and leapt out of bed.

"Damn, a leak!"

It seemed the rain had started falling from the ceiling onto his bed. He placed an empty mackerel can beneath the leak and lay down on the floor next to the bed. He curled his body inward and fell dead silent. We took turns sliding the shogi pieces away from the pile, listening to the raindrops dripping into the can. As the water accumulated, the pitch of the drops fell an octave.

"Damn, the roof needs fixin'!"

The soldier sprang up off the floor and stalked out of the infirmary. I worried his malaria would get worse if he went out in the rain but knew that trying to stop him wasn't going to do any good. For several moments, the raindrops falling into the tin echoed pleasantly. And then, we heard footsteps creaking on the roof. We turned our eyes up at the ceiling.

"The roof better not cave in," muttered the senior private.

The rain let up sometime before dusk.

I won the game of yamakuzushi that day. After Shimizu, without the use of his dominant hand, collapsed the pile of shogi pieces, I followed by picking up one of the pieces to earn the win.

A group of sickly soldiers had gathered around the hospital entrance. They were looking out at the courtyard, whispering something. We peered out over their backs. A soldier lay in a rain puddle reflecting the sunset. The malaria patient who'd gone out to fix the roof had fallen and died. "Maybe the enemy got him," someone whispered, while another guessed,

"Maybe he's just unconscious." The doctor checked the patient's pulse and pupils and confirmed he was dead. The medics cut off a finger and loaded the body onto a stretcher.

"Do you suppose this counts as a battle death?"

"Sure, he died on the battlefront, didn't he? Or, is it a disease-inflicted death?"

The can on the bed was now brimming with rainwater. Every time another drop fell, displaced water spilled out of the rusty can.

*

Oftentimes at the hospital, I woke up in the middle of the night. My nerves were always on alert; in an unexpected moment, I would stir awake. Once my slumber was interrupted, it was impossible to fall back to sleep, no matter how hard I tried. Rather than force myself, I would sit on a tree stump in the night breeze and occasionally look up at the stars. The stars were exceptionally beautiful after the rain. Their unsettling brilliance studded the dark and filled my vision.

The doctor had shown me how to find the Southern Cross once. First, you scan the Milky Way from the east and locate Rigel Kentaurus and Hadar in the Centaurus constellation. To the west was a dark patch almost empty of stars.

The doctor called this the "coal bag." If you looked west of the coal bag, you would find four brilliant dots. Oftentimes, I would connect the dots, drawing two lines with my finger. One line across, one line down.

We could not see the stars the night before the battle of Isurava. We were encamped on a mountain ledge, so our view of the sky was restricted. We had our heads so close together that we could hear each other breathing as we studied the map by candlelight.

We huddled beneath a canopy tent to keep the light from escaping. The tension stagnated in the cramped space. Sergeant Tanabe pointed to the mountain on the map with a pencil. We were told a plateau spread across the mountaintop. There, the Japanese forces in the northeast and the Australian forces in the southwest were deadlocked in a staring match. Our unit had been laying low in the southwest hillside behind the Australian position.

"The Japanese forces will attack come morning," explained Sergeant Tanabe, drawing a straight line from the Japanese position to the X marking the enemy position. "The enemy will likely pull back without mounting much of a counter attack, which has been their habit. And when they do …" He then drew a line from the X marking the enemy position to the X indicating ours. The sound of the pencil scratching

Finger Bone

against paper resounded. The sergeant directed his candlelit eyes at us. "We will engage the retreating forces here and take them out. We will commence digging encampments and fortify our positions. Know this: this is not a pincer attack. Steel yourselves well. You are to act in a manner befitting a soldier of the Imperial Army."

With that, he blew out the candle.

We worked up a sweat, digging the foxholes on the mountainside. The battleplan was indeed not a pincer attack. Our detachment comprised three squads, fewer than fifty men. We had been tasked with cutting off the retreat of a battalion. In short, we had borne the duty of dying.

Sergeant Tanabe was one of few senior officers I respected. When Fujiki died, the sergeant, like a true soldier, had put his hands together in prayer before his remains and wept. Though Tanabe was twenty-four and recently married, something about him suggested he was poised for death from the start. That resolve seemed to harden the farther we moved inland. Meanwhile, my own readiness was gradually shaken as I came to understand war. Though I'd believed myself ready to die, perhaps I had only thought so and nothing more. We'd heard the sergeant had volunteered us for the mission. Why did the sergeant, a man who had wept over Fujiki's death, send his own men into the jaws of death? I couldn't understand it at the time.

After I finished digging my foxhole, I went into the woods to take a leak. The trees tapered off immediately. Beyond the woods was a cliff which dropped into a yawning abyss expanding to the horizon. I heard a bird cry from somewhere below. It might have been a cassowary. I guessed the enormous bird with the red fleshy flap sagging from its throat might screech in just this way. The piss did not come right away. After I heard the cassowary's cry for a third or fourth time, the warm stream flowed down below.

When I returned to my foxhole, I began to shake. Though we were in the mountains, it was not cold; my body was sticky with sweat. I was shaking, unable to keep my teeth from chattering. I decided to have a smoke to clear my mind. My hands were trembling, and I had difficulty striking a match. Damp with my sweat, the match snapped in two. Upon the third try, the match head hissed to life, curling smoke up my nostrils. As my hand shook, so too did the flame. I brought my other trembling hand around it. When I inhaled the smoke, my molars quit chattering. When I lowered the cigarette from my lips, the chattering started again.

I crushed the butt against the dirt wall and reached for my cigarette pack. It was empty. I could do little else but stare at the dirt wall before me. So, there I stared, pouring sweat. Unpleasant thoughts invaded my mind. I imagined getting hit by

Finger Bone

shrapnel and dying, my bowels spilling out into the foxhole. Unconsciously, I put a hand on my belly. Feeling its warmth only intensified my trembling.

I leaned out of my foxhole to bum a cigarette. I called out to Furuya in the hole next to me. He was eating a can of salted beef.

"How can you eat that at a time like this?"

"Hey, we're all going to die in a couple of hours. I wanted to have the memory of what beef tasted like."

I grinned. "Is it any good?" Furuya grinned back. "My stomach's got the shakes. I can't taste a thing."

He tossed a pack of cigarettes at me. "You can have the rest."

With the pack in my hand, I went back to staring at the wall. I decided against smoking another. Like Furuya, I wasn't going to be able to taste a thing either. I leaned back on the wall and looked out of the hole. Next to the palm trees cutting across my view of the sky floated the moon. A full moon. The longer I stared at that flat circle, the more it resembled a human eye. It began to feel as though the yellow eye was looking down at me. I couldn't help but stare at it.

The moonlight waned as the sky whitened toward dawn. The moon became a dun-colored circle devoid of brilliance. And then, the *rat-tat-tat* of Type 99 light machine guns was heard. Sounds of shelling and grenade explosions rang out in succession. I grabbed a cartridge clip out of my ammo bag, loaded my rifle, and moved the bolt handle. The trembling had stopped. With death now bearing down upon us, I was eager for a fight. Sergeant Tanabe's readiness and mine were different. In that moment, I was not ready for death but had forgotten it entirely. That, too, was a way to steel yourself. The soldiers who'd lived their last moments in the foxholes had all steeled themselves, each in their own way, for what came next.

One night at the hospital, I heard a woman weeping.

I'd woken up in the middle of the night again and had been sitting on a tree stump, looking at the stars. I heard the faint voice of a woman crying in the night breeze. The wind threaded between the trees and drifted into the infirmary. I assumed it was the wind. I looked up at the stars again. The Southern Cross was low in the sky, and only the coal bag was visible among the scattered clouds. Then came the weeping again. I squinted toward the darkness between the trees. There was no one there. I listened intently and realized the weeping was not coming from the jungle but from the infirmary behind me. From somewhere near my bed.

And then, it made sense. It was my soul weeping for the sad bastard staring at the stars, alone, I thought. I went to the veranda, pulled back the shade, and peered inside.

Finger Bone

Sanada was curled in bed, weeping in the light of the moon. I took several breaths, unable to move. Finally, I let go of the shade and went back to the stump.

As I took in the night breeze, my heart was pounding.

Why had Sanada been weeping that night? I do not know. Nor will I ever.

It was evening, sometime after the string of rainy days. We picked up echoes of what sounded like gunfire coming from the south, from the direction of the Kanaka village. A group of wounded soldiers went out to the courtyard to investigate. "We must be fighting the Americans," the soldiers buzzed excitedly. The doctor, who did not seem particularly rattled, sent Sanada and me out to check it out. Shimizu asked to come along, and the three of us set off into the jungle.

We advanced about five hundred meters into the jungle when Shimizu let out a scream. I grabbed my rifle. Standing there was a familiar Kanaka from the village. He and Sanada proceeded to exchange a few words. I worried the village was being plundered by the Americans. We'd heard that some Americans had accused the people of one village of spying and had slaughtered them. "They put their hands on the girls, too," said a veteran soldier. "The Western savages must be driven out." The four of us made our way through the jungle toward the village. The closer we got to our destination, the more intense the booming became.

When we emerged from the jungle and came upon the clearing, it was my turn to scream. I dropped for cover. In the center of the clearing was a pillar of fire, around which a crowd of grotesque monsters writhed and danced. On second look, I realized they were human. They were wearing enormous painted masks, boldly colored decorations, their bodies covered in bark and leaves. Some of the black men were striking tubular drums with their hands. The peculiarly adorned humans danced around the fire to the drumbeat. Countless sparks crackled into the blue night.

A Kanaka man greeted us, "Nippon, heitai, jyoto," handed us wooden bowls, and filled them with palm wine. He passed us a tobacco roll measuring about thirty centimeters. One drag made my head spin. Sanada, as adaptable as ever, had drained his drink, smoked the tobacco, and was talking to the captain outside a nipa hut. When he returned, he explained, "They call this a sing-sing."

"Sing-sing?"

"It's just like it sounds in English. A celebration. The costumes represent the earth spirits. The captain said it's taboo to say any more about it to outsiders."

Around the fire were adults, children, and elders drinking

Finger Bone

palm wine, smoking the suspicious tobacco, and eating fruit. In one corner was a boiling pot giving off a strange smell. A couple of men were spooning meat from the pot onto flatbread made from sago palm starch. The Kanakas moved their lithe arms and legs to the drumbeat, bellowing and cawing like beasts and birds. Some were intoxicated by the wine and tobacco which were available in abundance.

As I watched the peculiar dance around the fire, drinking wine, listening to the drums and cries, an inexplicable fever filled my body. The drumming continued, its undulating rhythms echoing in the pit of my stomach. It felt as if I was listening to the music, not with my ears but with my belly. And with my belly attuned to the drumbeat, my body began to move, and before I knew it, Shimizu and I had tossed aside our rifles and were dancing with the others. The Kanakas had likely held these celebrations since time immemorial. Garish colors, primeval rhythms, a simple melody, memories from ancient times.

In that moment, I wept for the brothers I'd lost in battle. I did not cry after Fujiki's death. As I carried his body to the stream, I had fretted more about the prospect of my own death than I did his demise. I cried some in the foxhole after Sergeant Tanabe and Furuya died, but more from the bone-shattering pain that assaulted my body. Dancing as

I was now with tears in my eyes, the fire seemed to blur a more brilliant red. Shimizu also gave himself over to the fever, his forehead glittering with sweat, ranting, "When I saw my left hand lying on the ground, I wanted to die, but I'm glad I didn't. My left hand isn't me, and I'm not my left hand."

The tone of the music changed, prompting the black man next to me to take my hand. He gestured for me to do the same with the person on the other side of me. I made to take Shimizu's hand and, after a pause, held him below his elbow. Shimizu then held Sanada's hand to the right, and Sanada held the hand of the child next to him. We made a large circle around the fire and lost ourselves in the rhythms of the sing-sing. If the Americans had come to plunder the village at that moment, we might all been able to hold hands, made heady by palm wine and the warmth of the fire.

After giving ourselves over to the sing-sing for about half an hour, we recalled the doctor's orders and hastily retraced our steps back toward the hospital. The run through the jungle sobered us up. When we returned, everyone was taking a quiet dinner. The source of the noise wasn't an engagement with the enemy but drumming from a native festival, Sanada reported to the doctor, his breath stinking of drink. Grimacing, the doctor cautioned, "Best we don't intrude upon the native tribes without good reason," and retreated to the examination room. He was likely aware of Sanada and me visiting the village from time to time.

As impolite as it is to say, I didn't think the doctor was very suited to being a military officer. Nor was he suited to being a doctor at a sanatorium. He would do better as a doctor in a farming village. Marrying the sweet girl from the sanatorium and living out the rest of his life as a country doctor. That sounded to me like a terribly happy life.

After I ate dinner for a second time, I lay down on my bed with the excitement of the sing-sing still pulsing in me. The simple beat of the pig-skinned drum resounded in my body. It must have been the same for Sanada and Shimizu. We tossed and turned in our beds, and it wasn't until the night turned to day that we dropped off to sleep.

Several days later, after completing my morning exercises, I began to draw a map of the island on the ground with a branch to the best of my knowledge: the narrow peninsula said to stretch three hundred kilometers east and west, the Kumusi River running north and south inland, the mountain range near Isurava where I was wounded with Kagi, Nauro, and Ioribaiwa beyond that, as well as the American base on the western coast. Yet for the life of me, I could not ascertain the location of Field Hospital No. 3 on the island. I was certain I was wounded near Isurava but had been too groggy to gauge how long it'd taken to be transported to the tent hospital in the palm grove; nor did I know the route we'd taken to reach the field hospital. If by chance we'd taken a road I wasn't aware of, then there was no telling where I was on the island.

Exercising in the tranquil courtyard, soaking in the morning sun, I considered the possibility that the Greater East Asia War was already drawing to an end. The Imperial Navy had achieved a stunning victory in Midway in June and had inflicted heavy damage to the enemy base on Dutch Harbor. The islands of Kiska and Attu on the Aleutians were already under Imperial occupation. There was talk that air raids had commenced over Oregon, and that the rest of the US mainland was being razed to the ground by fire bombs. It was a plausible scenario if the Aleutian Islands were indeed under Imperial control. Or, perhaps the war had already entered peace talks. That the hospital was without a radio concerned me, as we would have to wait for a messenger to deliver such news. The prospect of languishing in the hospital without knowing the war had ended was no laughing matter.

"We might as well draw the Japanese islands."

Looking up, I found Sanada stooping a few meters way, drawing an outline of Kyushu with a branch. He drew Shikoku, Honshu, and Hokkaido next. Then Karafuto, Okinawa, and the Ogasawara Islands. I drew the equator line above the island I'd drawn. Drawing the map made apparent how close we were to the edge of the world.

Suddenly, I heard the echoes of what sounded like bubbles bursting. I thought I'd imagined it at first until I heard two more pops. They were different from the drumbeats of the Kanaka village. Tossing aside his stick, Sanada got up and looked skyward. I did the same. We heard the wind sigh, the tree branches rustle—and then, *pop, pop*!

I wondered if it was a sound of the natural world, but I detected a ring of intent. The popping echoed in succession, then a period of silence, and then the popping again. It was a human-made sound. As my ears became accustomed to the distant sounds, I was able to pick them up more distinctly.

His eyes searching the sky, Sanada muttered, "Artillery fire."

He was right. If my memory served me correctly, it was the sound of Type 41 mountain guns.

Shimizu came down with malarial fever for a third time.

His temperature had spiked, and when it exceeded forty degrees, he fell into an altered state of consciousness and then into a coma. "He may not come out of this one," said the doctor, smiling sadly. He stroked his beard and sighed.

After a couple of days, Shimizu regained consciousness and went back to sketching as if nothing had happened.

Since the sing-sing, Shimizu had taken an interest in the Kanakas, so I told him stories about the village while I sharpened his pencil. "They're learning Japanese. Do you know what they're aiming to do? They're going to make a haul taking the Japanese sightseeing." Nodding, Shimizu ran his pencil across the paper then stopped to look me in the eye.

"Do me a favor? Will you take me back to the village?"

Shimizu's look surprised me. An odd vitality lit his eyes like an illumination reflecting in a marble. I'd seen this in others in the past. Humans are strange creatures: they seem to regain their senses momentarily before death takes them.

The wound in his left leg had gotten worse, making it difficult for Shimizu to walk on his own. I talked to the doctor about it, and he loaned us some crutches. Thanking me, Shimizu stuck the crutches under his arms and got up from his bed. One of the crutches fell slowly to the ground, and Shimizu fell back on his rear. Without his left hand, he wasn't able to hold the handle of the crutch. He didn't realize it himself until the crutch toppled over.

"I guess we can take turns carrying him," said Sanada, sitting next to Shimizu.

We played rock, paper, scissors, and it was decided I would

carry him first. I squatted before the bed and put him on my back. I stood up, supporting his rear, and nearly gasped. He weighed nothing on my back. I was able to support him easily with one arm. Shimizu was certainly skinny, but he must have weighed thirty or forty kilograms. I hardly felt the burden of his weight on my back. He wrapped his good arm and his nub of an arm around my neck. He smelled faintly of herbs. A sweet smell similar to jasmine. Perhaps that was how the body smelled when the malaria mixed with the medicines and antiseptics.

Once we were halfway through the jungle, it was Sanada's turn to carry him. I walked a bit behind, staring at Shimizu's rounded back. He reminded me of a cicada husk. A husk as thin as celluloid, the color of cinnamon candy. Not that Shimizu was a husk. He was alert and talking lucidly, in fact. Still, the image lingered and would not leave me. Perhaps it was because the cicada husk I'd found in a coastal pine forest long ago had a rounded back like it was holding on to something. And then, I recalled the time Shimizu was unusually talkative. When was it? The freshly washed, crisp, sundried uniform … it was on the walk back after we'd skipped rocks at the creek. He had walked ahead of Sanada and me, tossing a stone he'd picked up at the creek and turned around from time to time.

"The truth is I wanted to study at the Imperial Art School

in Kichijoji. Not because I wanted to be an artist, I like to draw, you know? I just like to draw."

There was a break in the trees and the dappled sun fell over us. The sunlight and shadows played on Shimizu's rounded back like a kaleidoscope.

When we reached the clearing of the village, the young men gathered around and greeted us, "Nippon, heitai, jyoto." Sanada pointed to Shimizu on his back and said, "We'd like to show him around the village." One of the men turned around and went down on his haunches. He was offering to carry Shimizu himself and take him around. With Shimizu now perched on his back, he climbed up the hill leading deeper into the village. Sanada and I took a seat on a log and waited for them to return.

"He may not have much longer."

I did not know what the malaria parasite looked like. From the kanji character for "insect" in its name, I imagined a creature like a measuring worm. Like a measuring worm sizing up its habitat, the parasites crawled inside Shimizu's blood vessels, devouring the red blood cells. The red blood cells were being riddled with holes, like worm-eaten leaves which you can see through to the other side. Why did the malaria parasite try to kill its host, I couldn't understand. If Shimizu died, the parasites would lose its food source and die too.

Finger Bone

Before long, the black man returned with Shimizu. Shimizu sat down on the log and took out a tinplate and a pad of paper. He then put his pencil to work. Holding the paper in place with his bandaged nub, he sketched line after line without a moment's hesitation. The villagers gathered round and peered in, chattered something, then laughed. As he continued to draw like a man possessed, the spirited chatter turned to murmurs, and then silence. We watched quietly until the sketch was finished.

Shimizu drew a woman boiling copra in a pot, drew a child smoking a cigarette, drew the nipa huts standing along the slope. Next, he drew a black pig sleeping belly-up under the eaves. I looked alternately at the pig in front of me and the image being sketched on the pad. More than drawing its likeness, Shimizu appeared to be committing the beating parts of the pig onto the page. I wondered if the real pig might die when Shimizu was finished. Shimizu did finish, turned the page, and immediately set to work on the next sketch. The real pig was asleep, its pot belly rising and falling.

When he filled all ten of the pages of the pad, he looked up and took a breath. Only then did he realize the villagers gathered around him. The elderly captain of the village said something excitedly. Shimizu turned to Sanada.

"He wants to know if he can have the drawings."

Shimizu gave the elder all of the drawings he'd made. Taking them, the captain hurried back to the nipa hut, the rings of his staff clanging noisily. He returned with a mountain of bananas in his arms. Sanada, Shimizu, and I sat on the grass and feasted on the sweet fruit to our hearts' content, taking what we couldn't finish back to the infirmary.

That evening Shimizu took his last breath.

I don't know what became of those drawings. Perhaps they're hanging in someone's nipa hut. Perhaps they were used for rolling tobacco.

Days after Shimizu died, I went fishing with Sanada. We walked along the creek until it swelled to a width such that it could properly be called a river. Several rocks big enough to accommodate a human peeked out of the surface. We sat cross-legged on the rocks and dangled our lines. The fishing poles were fashioned by tying a vine to a bamboo stick. We used dried twigs as floats and kneaded rice with water for bait. We did not talk, only dangled our lines and passed the time.

The sound of the river seemed constant, and yet it wasn't. The sound of water slipping over the rocks, of moss-covered twigs being swept away, stones tumbling along the river bottom, bubbles rising to the surface and bursting. A multitude of sounds converged to orchestrate the hum of the river. No two sounds were alike, and yet they sounded as if they were. As I listened to that hum, it began to sound as if it were coming from inside me. As if the water was also flowing inside my body. But if the sound was coming from within, I might never reach its source. Why I heard the water in this way, I did not know. I was dead inside. Dead, and yet strangely at peace. We didn't catch any fish that day.

A cavernous hole seemed to have opened up inside me. I did not feel sadness. Death had become commonplace. Sergeant Tanabe died, Fujiki died, and Furuya died at the battle of Isurava. Patients died every day at the hospital. The jazz singer, the skilled shogi player, the kokeshi doll maker had all died. I did not feel sadness. However, I did perceive a thin line dangling in the pit of my soul. I knew it was there because it rang from time to time. Something was tied to the end of it. It was not an abstraction but something I'd seen in reality. Gazing at the palmwood ceiling from my bed, I tried to think of what was tied to the end of that line. The answer did not come to me.

Sanada and I continued to visit the Kanaka village often. Sanada found the Kanaka language interesting. "If you throw English, German, and French in a pot, boil them down, and sprinkle in some palm wine, then you've got the Kanaka language," he said. I had little interest in the language or in teaching the Kanakas. So, I sat on the grass atop the hill and watched him teach. He held forth, mixing exaggerated gestures. The stalwart men looked up at him, with rapt attention, their faces child-like. They appeared smaller than they were.

One afternoon, I sat at my usual spot on the grass, and a villager came up the hill. It was the young man named Munini who'd carried Shimizu on his back. He sat down next to me and began talking. I couldn't understand what he was saying. His tone and breaths between words suggested he was making a heartfelt declaration about something. His body trembled slightly. I patted his back, and Munini let slip a sob. I sensed he was talking about the people he'd lost. My friends died by the American bombs, he might have said. That's why we remain friendly toward the Japanese. I will never forgive the Americans.

I answered in Japanese, "The Americans will pay for their wanton bombings. I'll avenge your friends' deaths one day."

Munini turned toward me. He whimpered, "Jyoto," and a tear rolled down his black cheek.

One early afternoon, a severe dysentery patient, who'd been passing blood in his stool, died in bed. The medic cut off the deceased's flesh and bone. When I heard the blade come down upon the cutting board, something tinkled inside me. Then I understood. The thing tied to the end of the thin line was a goldfish-patterned wind chime hanging in the window of my parents' home.

It was around this time that Sanada fell ill with the local disease.

*

And then, I thought. And then, my gaze fell on the sunlight hitting my left leg just below the knee. I stared at the sun-drenched leg as if I were gazing at a distant landscape. The blood circulated to my calf, my ankle, to the back of the foot. The blood warmed by the sun's heat coursed and made its way up until I felt it. That was how I knew the leg belonged to me.

How much time had passed since I'd rested my back against the tree, with the steel cylinder in my hand? The tree's shadow stretched toward the yellow road. Judging from its length, I guessed it was about three. If it was three on the is-land, it would have just passed noon in Japan. About the time adults and children, the elderly and babies—everyone would be having lunch. Though the island was hot year-round, it would be winter in Japan. My hometown would be bound in snow and fog. A fire burning in the dusty lumpen stove in the corner of the living room. Chizuru might be heating dried mochi on it.

My left leg cleared the shadow of the tree. The kneecap rose into relief. My blood coursed. And then, I thought. The rainy days passed, patients died, we fished in a fishless creek, and then …

Sanada was in bed being examined by the doctor. He complained of a painful itch on his back. I watched his shirt being pulled up and shuddered. A rash of irregular shapes and sizes spread across his back. A rash was common in dengue fever, with relatively uniform and small lesions. However, the lesions on Sanada's back were swollen, some as big as three centimeters. The doctor handed Sanada some mercurochrome solution and said, "We'll try this, then we wait and see." I knew what this disease was. The doctor, too. I'd seen patients with the same red rash when I was first brought to the infirmary. They all died. Their bodies became covered with lesions, the whites of their eyes turning the color of blood, and when their temperature exceeded forty degrees, they suffered an inflamed brain and died in a seizing fit. The doctor said it was an unknown disease that was reported soon after the frontline extended to the South Seas. High

Finger Bone

fever, rash, non-transmissible by humans—that was the extent of what was known about the disease.

"That there are Japanese on this island at all is extraordinary. Maybe something extraordinary will happen to the virus inside a Japanese body."

That afternoon, Sanada and I went back to the Kanaka village. We sat on the grassy hill and gazed at the nipa huts along the slope. As was the case when we'd gone fishing, we hardly exchanged words. I tried to say something, but every attempt ended in a sigh. I could have said anything, I suppose, but the words shriveled into air by some unseen power.

Sometime later, the Kanaka man with the machete approached, bearing coconuts. Sticking the machete in the ground, he held a coconut each in his right hand and left hand and began talking cheerfully. He gestured like he was cutting one open and drinking the juice, and after wiping his mouth with the back of a hand, he flashed his white teeth. I guessed he was trying to sell them to us. Sanada took out some shell money, but the man shook his head. He skillfully cut open the coconuts with the machete and started back down the hill. Sanada and I exchanged a look, then took the coconuts in our hands.

The juice was sweet and a bit salty and did well to quench our thirst. Resting the coconut on my belly, I leaned back and stared up at the western sky. A bird sat on the roof of a nipa hut, watching us. Its handsome yellow tailfeathers drooped over the side of the palmwood roof. After a while, Sanada brought up the subject of his son.

"My boy's name is Kotaro."

"Oh?" I waited a bit, but Sanada did not reply. "Were you the one to name him?"

"It was my wife. She'd decided on Kotaro if it was a boy and Sanae if it was a girl before the baby was born. She kept saying it was a girl because the baby wasn't kicking inside, but when the baby was born, we checked between his legs. He was a boy alright."

"What does your wife do?" I asked before remembering she'd died.

Seemingly mishearing the question, he answered, "We were substitute teachers at the elementary school. We promised to marry when the cherry blossoms were in bloom, and we did."

It was the first time I learned Sanada was a teacher. I questioned whether he was suited to being an educator but thought he would be well-liked by the children. I imagined him being called "sensei" by adoring students and almost became jealous. I imagined the couple standing face-to-face beneath the cherry blossoms, her eyes looking down at the pink scattered about the schoolyard. A young, healthy woman who gave birth to a boy only to die of consumption in a hospital bed with her husband at her side. It was a bad habit running my imagination in this way. Running my imagination caused the thin line to tremble. It trembled until I was powerless to do anything. My grandfather had bought me that glass wind chime years ago at an obon festival. With my right hand clutching a cotton candy and left hand holding the wind chime, I had looked up at the enormous yellow chrysanthemum flower appearing as if it might lose its shape and fall from the night sky.

Rubbing his bandaged eye, Sanada continued, "You ever watch a baby being born?"

"Can't say that I have."

"My wife was as calm as could be, but me? I couldn't believe that another human could come out of a person. Couldn't get my head around it, even though it's the most natural thing in the world. I paced the halls of the hospital ward, talking to myself. Rambling about how the baby's name was Kotaro, how he was born between my wife and me, how that would make me his father. I must have done fifty trips up and down the halls before I was able to touch his hand and watch him sleeping next to her. His hand didn't feel human, more like a plump bit of fat that happened to be shaped like a hand by accident. When I touched his hand, it felt like a miracle."

"I don't have any kids, so I guess I wouldn't know anything about that."

"You will someday."

"Yeah, if we ever make it back home."

"You will."

"There's no telling who gets to go home alive."

"You will."

There the conversation ended. So too did my imagination. I watched the Kanaka going about their daily lives, listening to the water splash inside the coconut shell. Black bodies moved about the clearing below. They tilled the fields, raised pigs and chickens, and grew sago palm. It was strange to see people making a life in a remote jungle thousands of kilometers away from Japan. The bird on the roof was gone. I'd missed seeing it fly away, so it seemed as if the bird had simply slipped to the other side of the roof.

A group of children scampered up the hill toward us. They said something in the Kanaka language. Sanada ripped some pages out of his notebook and began folding them into paper airplanes, with the children crowded around him.

"This is a Zero, this is a Spitfire, and this is a Lockheed P-38. Now, which do you think will fly the farthest?"

He rose to his feet, pinched the body of one plane, and brought it level with his face. For a moment, he paused. He was reading the wind. And then, making up his mind, he traced an arc with his fingers and launched the plane into the sky. Buffeted by the wind, the plane wobbled and teetered quite a distance before landing in the grass. The children chased after it, chirping like birds.

Looking on, Sanada said, "You'll have to introduce me to Chizuru-chan when we get home."

"Not a chance. I'm not letting a bum like you near my little sister."

"Come on, I'll introduce you to a nurse I know. The nurses at the Red Cross are angels."

Sanada picked up another plane and searched for the optimal angle from which to launch it. Lifting his heels slightly off the ground, he turned his shoulders and flicked his wrist just before his arm attained full extension. The plane caught a breeze and lofted away.

Watching Sanada carrying on, I knew he sensed death was imminent.

Sanada was able to move for several days afterward. Though his appetite had dropped, he could still eat rice gruel. "I've got the chills like the spirit world has got a hold of me," he said, his fingers quivering as he ate. Eating gruel, Sanada didn't look like himself. I took my meal, facing the other direction.

The bed in front of me was empty, and since Shimizu died, so was the one beyond it. I shoveled the food into my mouth, looking at the empty beds.

One night, Sanada's temperature began to rise, and by the next morning, it had climbed to forty degrees. The pain in his joints kept him from being able to stand, and he fell in and out of consciousness. He babbled incoherently, delirious with fever. At times, his breathy exhalations mixed with moans, and the moans mixed with words. Though most of it was gibberish, occasionally enough words were strung together to be intelligible. He seemed to be recalling his childhood and life back in Japan. He seemed to be seeing something I couldn't. One time, my name came up in his ramblings, which startled me. I seemed to have made an appearance in his dreams. I froze in my bed for a moment. Then, Sanada inhaled deeply and went back to rambling.

I passed several sleepless nights contemplating the stars. I didn't bother locating the Southern Cross. I simply gazed at the constellations scattered beyond the black jungle, hearing Sanada's moans, knowing this time the voice was his rather than that of a phantom woman. At times, the stars flickered on and off. Every time Sanada moaned, the yellow lights faded, and when he stopped, the lights blinked back on. Seeing as the stars were incapable of picking up the human voice,

Finger Bone

it had to be a figment of my imagination. When the coal sack was directly above my head, I went back to bed, surrendering to something.

Sanada's condition declined rapidly. The red lesions multiplied and spread over the healthy skin. His throat hurt too much to swallow the rice gruel. He hardly drank any water. The swelling of the lymph nodes in his neck were visible under the bandages.

The doctor came around to his bed with a can of mandarin oranges. Sanada put two slices in his mouth, then shook his head. The doctor went back to the examination room, nodding to himself. I could do nothing for Sanada. I lay in bed and watched him getting weaker.

"Is the fever making you hot?"

A corporal placed a damp towel on Sanada's forehead. I'd not seen the two talking before. Perhaps the corporal was suffering from brain fever, too. He sat on Sanada's bed and fanned him with a paper fan, muttering, "Gettin' smaller. From my view, from your view. Gettin' smaller, but only *looks* smaller."

The following morning, edema started to appear on his face and feet. His bandaged face swelled like an enormous blister. Though he was unconscious, he occasionally gasped in pain. The doctor tapped a finger against his forehead, repeating helplessly, "What to do ..." Sanada's organs were failing. He received injections of normal saline and Ringer's solution every few hours, but the infirmary lacked the medicines he needed most. A little after noon, I watched the doctor give him a shot of morphine hydrochloride, and I knew nothing more could be done.

Around two in the afternoon, I was staring at the palm-wood ceiling from my bed when Sanada called my name. I suspected it was just his fever talking, but he called me again. When I peered over at him, he lifted his swollen eyelids covered with lesions and looked at me, his eyes glassy like crystal orbs.

"I'd like some water. Would you bring me some water from the creek?"

"Sure. I'll go right now."

There was drinking water in the bucket, but Sanada wanted a clean, cold drink right out of the creek. I grabbed my mess tin and bolted out the door.

Outside there were wounded soldiers exercising as usual, stretching and constricting their limbs slowly. A malaria patient was sunbathing on the bench. Two yellow butterflies fluttered about him. I blew past the tranquil scene and set off down the trail. As I ran through the jungle, myriad images

Finger Bone

flashed through my head: my father wolfing down the red bean rice, the pod of dolphins seen from the ship's watch-tower, Furuya listening to the waves, Shimizu eating his meals on the floor on his knees, and Sanada proudly teaching Japanese to the Kanakas. I shook them off and cut through the shafts of light crisscrossing the jungle, the mess tin squeaking in my hand.

I came upon the hill behind the vegetable field and heard the hum of the creek. I raced down the grassy hill, my weight back on my heels, then stopped. I held my breath. There was a group of Americans near the creek. I made myself small and hid in the tall grass. I dropped on my belly, as sweat shot out of every pore.

I parted the grass in front of me and looked down upon the creek. The soldiers were congregating at the water's edge, taking a drink of water, smoking. One soldier was standing on the fallen tree, taking a piss. They were talking loudly in English, armed with carbines, not a bit of dirt on their uniforms. If the frontline had advanced beyond Isurava, as I'd guessed, they were likely stragglers caught in Japanese-controlled territory. Although, hiding in the grass as I was, dripping with sweat with only a mess tin in my possession, I looked more like a straggler than they did.

With one hand still clenching the bundle of grass before

me, I waited for the enemy soldiers to leave. The water was there in front of me, yet I could not fetch it. Sanada didn't have long. Once the eyes turned glassy, it was a lost cause. Watching so many patients die around me, I understood why the eyes turned the way they did. The dying person became devoid of every human desire they once possessed. Having nothing more to communicate, their voices turned gentle, their eyes limpid, their senses lucid, as they quietly and slowly approached death. I noticed blood seeping from the bundle of grass. I opened my hand to find dozens of red slashes on my fingers.

After some time, the Americans moved off and disappeared, their sing-song English echoing downstream. I poked my head out of the grass, and after making certain they were out of sight, I ran down the hill and dipped my mess tin in the creek. Then I ran back into the jungle with my mess tin heavy with cold water.

When I returned to the infirmary, the doctor and a medic were standing around Sanada's bed. Upon seeing me dripping with sweat, holding my mess tin, the doctor acknowledged me with a nod. I did not know what the nod meant. I found Sanada lit by the faint light filtering in from the grass shade. His face was covered in bandages, so I couldn't get a look at his complexion. I turned to the doctor, but he was looking down at the patient. The medic, too. That was how I knew Sanada had taken his last breath.

On the day of my grandfather's funeral, I had stood at the entrance of the family altar room in much the same way. I was in elementary school. My father was stooped over the coffin, dabbing my grandfather's grey lips with a damp cotton pad. The brown cicadas chirred endlessly in the trees. My mother next to me prompted, "Now you give your grandfather a drink of water." I was scared to look at my grandfather's dead body. Scared to see the man, who used to box my ears, all made up and stuffed inside a coffin filled with cut chrysanthemums.

I asked the doctor for a dressing pad. I picked it up with forceps and dipped it in the cool water in the mess tin. I removed the bandages around Sanada's mouth and dabbed the water on his lips.

"Does this count as having given him a drink of water?" I asked.

"That's a matter of how you feel," answered the doctor. "The dead can't speak for themselves, so I suppose it's up to the interpretation of the living."

One of the medics came around with a plywood board and a knife. He laid the board on the bed and Sanada's hand on top of it. Taking the hand by the thumb and laying it flat, he placed the knife at the base of the thumb and brought his weight down upon the blade. He wrapped the severed digit in a dressing.

"May I have the bone after you've burned off the flesh?"

The medic's eyes widened, then immediately softened into a gentle smile.

"Of course. Your friend will be glad, I'm sure. There's no telling who'll be able to go back to the homeland."

The medics carried Sanada on a stretcher up the hillside pointing toward the pallid summer sky. It was a treacherous trek to reach the vista, but the medics had likely dug a hole there in view of the field of flowers that resembled moonflowers. They climbed halfway up the hill and set down the stretcher. Sanada disappeared in the flowers. The pink petals swayed as if they were singing. There appeared to be male flowers and female flowers. The male flower draped its petals outward, while the female flower was shaped like a crumpled ball of tissue paper. One medic held Sanada by the wrists, while the other held him by his ankles. His body was lifted out of the flowers. They swung him this way and that way, and with the third swing, Sanada disappeared into the flowers for good. The medics looked down into the hole for a good while. I looked up at the hill of moonflowers for a good while. I brought my hands together in prayer and noticed the pain in my shoulder was gone.

Finger Bone

One afternoon, I lay in bed, contemplating the three-cen-timeter bone in the palm of my hand. It was shaped like a horsetail shoot. It smelled faintly of roasted beans. My palm was sweating. The tiny droplets flickered silver in the sunlight. The bone rested on the palm like it was taking a nap.

"How did you know you were going to die?"

The bone did not answer.

If Sanada were around, he might have answered that a lit-tle bird had told him.

After Sanada's death, the days passed in idleness. I ate, exer-cised, worked in the field, ate again, and slept. I had become a "tourist" of the kind Ichimura had spoken of. The days might have been described as halcyon. The wounded continued to die one by one, and one by one, the empty beds became more numerous. A halcyon time during which humans slow-ly wasted away and died.

I went to the Kanaka village exactly once after Sanada died. When I stepped foot in the clearing, no one came to greet me, Nippon, heitai, jyoto. Perhaps the villagers were working in the fields. There were only a few Kanaka men in the clearing, no women or children. I decided to take a stroll through the village.

On top of the slope on the north end of the village was a

hut of odd construction. Part of the roof was made of palm fronds twisted into the shape of towers. Numerous shells hung on the walls, and the entrance was covered with two layers of grass shades. I peered between the slits and glimpsed several severed heads arranged in a line. A second look revealed they were wooden masks. Painted black and adorned with feathers and palm fronds, they were ones that had been used at the sing-sing.

A black man grabbed me by the shoulder from behind. He spoke emphatically, but I couldn't understand what he was saying. He was clearly angry about something. Despite my irritation at being berated without reason, I backed out of the hut without a fuss. It appeared I had become an unwelcome guest to the inhabitants of the village. I descended the slope back down to the clearing where a couple of black pigs rambled in the grass. I left the Kanaka village, listening to the pigs grunting at my back.

After returning to the infirmary, I lit a cigarette beneath the tree in the courtyard. I watched the plumes of smoke disappear into the dappled sunlight, snuffed out the cigarette, and tossed it. And then, I must have nodded off. When I opened my eyes, half of my body was baking in the sun. The crushed cigarette lay in a V on the ground. Several meters beyond it in the middle of the courtyard was a fallen tree in

Finger Bone

decay. A tiny branch sprouted up from the trunk toward the sky, the space above it breaking into colors like three paints dropped on a palette. The colors swirled clockwise and began to take the shape of a creature. Stuck in my slumber, I could not make out what it was.

The head was a yellow the shade of tropical flowers, the throat a deep marine blue, and magnificent red tail feathers nearly touched the ground. The creature seemed to embody all the colors of the island. A bird-of-paradise, I muttered in my head. The bird did not notice me. Its head was tilted toward the western hill where the dead were buried. Careful not to make a sound, I picked up the rifle I'd propped against the tree and pulled the bolt handle. I moved the barrel slowly until the muzzle was pointed at the bird. The rifle was not loaded, but that didn't matter. The Kanakas worshipped spirits, and the creature before me seemed to be of a similar kind.

I set the bird in the sights of the rifle, and it seemed to exist not on the branch several meters away but inside the one-centimeter diameter circle. If I reached out my hand, I might be able to touch the tiny bird confined inside the circle. There were times during shooting practice when I would hit the target, yet other times I would miss even when the target was in my sights. I'd always wondered what accounted for the different outcomes. Perhaps if I set the target inside myself rather than in the sights, I would be able capture it. I squeezed the trigger.

A dry crack rang out. I raised my head. The bird was no longer there. It was spreading its enormous red wings about two meters away from the branch. With several flaps of its wings, it ascended above the roof of the infirmary. After circling the ultramarine sky, it soared past the hill where the dead were buried and beyond until it was a speck of a shadow. It disappeared into the horizon.

One morning, life in the field hospital ended abruptly.

I was sitting in bed, bending and stretching my arm now unencumbered by the sling. I was able to extend my arm flat without any pain. A cacophony of footsteps and panting approached from outside the infirmary. I grabbed my rifle and took a peek through the slits of the grass shade. A number of black-faced ghosts wavered in the courtyard. A closer look revealed they were Japanese soldiers. They were skin and bones, their uniforms torn, their faces like death masks, swaying in the blinding sun.

The medics went around and passed out oatmeal to the soldiers. Some ate ravenously; others stared vacantly into their mess tin lids. A lid fell out of a soldier's hand, the gruel dribbling onto the dry earth. I glimpsed a fly perched on the soldier's eye and knew he was already dead.

Finger Bone

With the arrival of the lost soldiers, the smell of the infirmary changed. Gone was the dry smell of death mixed with ethanol and drugs. The place was filled with the stench of decaying flesh that clung to the skin.

The floorboards of the entrance creaked. Backlit in the doorway stood a cadaverous man who appeared to be an officer. He looked across at the wounded in bed and let out a shrill voice reminiscent of a longhorn beetle's cry.

"The entire eastern coast—Buna, Giruwa, and the Basabua regions—have fallen under Allied control. We will board a Daihatsu-class landing craft and divert north up the Kumusi River and on to Salamaua. All able-bodied men will prepare to depart at once."

The announcement set everyone astir. Saying nothing more, the cadaverous officer exited the infirmary, with an odd lightness in his step. The officer had refrained from saying "retreat," some semblance of military discipline still holding the corpse of a man together.

I'd conjectured that the western coast might already be under Imperial occupation, but that had turned out to be an illusion. If the Buna region was under Allied control, then the frontline was not merely being pushed back but was well behind us. It also meant Field Hospital No. 3 existed beyond the frontline, like an isolated island.

Many of the patients were not ambulatory. The fever patients were in a semi-conscious state, and the dysentery patients were too emaciated to stand. One soldier without a leg shouldered his rucksack and left the infirmary on crutches, only to return and lie back down on his bed. After some deliberation, he had likely come to the conclusion that he would not be able to survive the jungle on one leg.

The doctor who'd been occupied in the examination room came out to the infirmary. He looked around at the wounded, let out a short, deep breath, and spoke in the dignified voice of a soldier.

"You'll find several days of foodstuff and some medicine in the examination room. As a soldier and as a doctor, it gives me no pleasure to leave you behind."

The medics went around and distributed grenades for the purpose of committing suicide. The soldiers who were conscious were handed the steel cylinders directly. A grenade was left next to the pillows of the unconscious soldiers. Though they were instruments of death, the steel lumps appeared as though they were the souls of the soldiers lying next to them. The medics' silhouettes rose into relief against the sun and closed in on me. A critical patient with dysentery said from his bed, "Glad to see you're being discharged." I turned to him and saw he wasn't being sarcastic. He'd merely spoken what was in his heart. As my senses became uncommonly lucid, I stuffed my meager belongings into my rucksack.

On my way out, the drawing inscribed *A Soldier Eating* caught my attention. I put a hand on it, intending to take all of the drawings down. But my hand went no further. The drawings weren't meant to be taken by the departing; they were meant to remain with those being left behind until the end, if not longer. Letting go of the edge of the drawing, I took a final look at the image of the eating solder and went out to the courtyard.

The invalid men were about to depart. They marched unsteadily into the jungle. The doctor and I fell in line behind the last man. I turned around at the jungle's entrance and cast a look at the field hospital. The building stood in the brilliance of the morning sun. It was quiet. The wounded soldiers lay in bed on the other side of the grass shades. Grasping their grenades, waiting for the moment to pull the pin. Glad to see you're being discharged.

I did not turn around again.

A formation of American aircraft flew through the sky and the woolly clouds.

I watched the bellies of the aircraft disappear behind the vegetation giving me cover. The rumble of the engines shook the leaves. And just as quickly as it came, the rumble faded and became more distant. Why weren't the Curtis fighters attacking us? If one of the white-scarved fighter pilots put a bullet in me, it would save me from having to use the grenade in my hand.

I heard another thud somewhere down the yellow road. Someone had dropped dead from the breeze caused by the flyby. That was all it took for the last thin line to break. Perhaps the thin line was more like a dotted line. A dotted line, which at some point, had ceased to dot.

I tapped against my ribcage and heard a hollow sound. The echo of water. I'd heard that water accumulates in the belly with the onset of starvation. How did the water accumulate when one hadn't had a drop of water? I tapped against my belly repeatedly, thirsting for the water inside.

The first few days after departing the infirmary, we maintained a line. Though we were a makeshift group of the sick and wounded, we continued to function as a military unit. But when our food supply was exhausted, that discipline grew lax. Some of the soldiers used their suicide grenades to catch fish. They threw them into a lake, bringing fish resembling bass and mackerel floating belly up to the surface. The soldiers devoured the fish greedily. The next morning, they were all dead. To men who'd subsisted on nothing but plants, meat and fish were the equivalent of poison.

It was not long before we lost our rifles. The nights were cold in the mountains, even in the South Seas. The cold could kill the weakened soldiers. You were liable to freeze to death on an island of perpetual summer. The area was sprawling with exposed rock, and there was nothing that could be used as firewood. Some soldiers tried to start a fire with the few plants growing among the rocks, but the plants burnt to ash in an instant. We huddled together beneath the tent, shivering. And then, someone realized the stocks of our rifles were made of wood. Someone else joked, "If we use the wooden bits to build a fire, you can bet our hands would be nice and warm." The others chuckled, but their eyes weren't laughing. We tossed our rifles on the fire. One soldier stirred the ashes with the barrel of his rifle, and something inside the fire popped spitting sparks up into the dark. "You will all be executed by order of court-martial for rendering the Emperor's rifle to ash," raged the senior private, but his rifle was also among the ash in the fire. Our bodies did not move as we wished. Our thoughts and actions became mixed up. I recalled a marionette of a clown I'd happened upon in a toy store window as a child. The body was moved by strings attached to its hands and feet. At one point, I became mixed up. Before I was cognizant of my actions, I had thrown both my ammo bags into the valley below. After watching the bags and loose rocks tumble into the darkness, I jerked my head up. I hallucinated an enormous pair of hands floating above me. But there was only the pristine sky expanding over the mountain range.

The doctor did his best to look after the invalid soldiers, but once the medical supplies ran out, he could do little more than take their pulse. "I'm no longer an army doctor or any kind of doctor, but an ordinary man," said the doctor, smiling sadly. The doctor was not to blame, of course. Perhaps this too was owing to impotence. At some point, he broke from the line and ambled down to the creek alone. A short time later, a shot rang out, scaring a flock of birds into flight. I went to investigate and found the doctor had shot himself in the head with a pistol. Though the heart had probably stopped pumping, black blood was still trickling from the tiny hole in his head. The bullet had gone through the right temple, but there was blood was dripping out of his left ear.

I crouched next to him and touched the pistol in his hand. The pistol would come in handy in a trade with the other starving soldiers. The doctor's hand was seized in rigor mortis, and I could not wrest the gun from his grip. The index finger, which was bent into the shape of a hook, was caught in the trigger guard. I unsheathed my bayonet and put the blade on the base of his finger. A sliver of light bounced off the blade and blinded me for an instant. When I opened my eyes, I glimpsed my deformed reflection in the blade. It was then I realized that I was acting out of sorts. I put away the bayonet and shook my head. I shook my head repeatedly, and then the figure of the girl taking open-air therapy in the courtyard floated to mind. When I came to my senses, I was stacking stones next to the doctor's body, like a child on the Sai-no-Kawara beach. Afterward, I took a long drink of water from the creek until I could drink no more.

After the river and mountain crossings, the march continued across flat jungle terrain. Along the way, I encountered a Kanaka village in the valley. I thought I was saved. Memories of my adventures with the Kanakas came back to me, and the greeting *apinun* filled me with fondness. I imagined taro, bananas, and mango, causing my stomach to churn. A black man with a rifle spotted me and let out an inhuman cry. He started shooting. He was wearing a short-sleeved shirt and shorts. A bullet ricocheted off the palm tree next to me. I didn't know what in hell was happening. I had already pictured myself saying *kai kai* and patting my belly to gesture for food. One by one, more black men appeared, squawking like birds, firing their rifles. I fled into the jungle, in a state of confusion.

Why were they shooting? Were they the rumored savage headhunting tribe? Why were headhunters armed with rifles? I couldn't make sense of any of it. Their wrathful howls and bellows, their trampling footfalls preyed after me. I was more afraid of being captured than I was of being shot dead. If they were indeed the rumored savage tribe, they were likely to commit a brutal killing, to kill a man by primitive means. They might saw off my head with a dull, corroded machete. Nearly tearing up in horror, I recalled the soldier I'd shot.

There was no denying I shot a young Australian soldier near Isurava. I aimed for the chest, but the barrel had jerked back due to the pain in my shoulder, and the bullet bore into the base of his white neck. An alarming amount of blood had spouted like a fountain, raining black blood all over the grass. The bullet had blown a hole in the trachea, and a high-pitched whistle rang out in the glow of the setting sun. Looking vacantly in the air, he pressed his hand against the base of his neck spraying blood and fell over backward. My trigger finger tingled as proof of the killing. As I was being treated the following day, I noticed the body of the white soldier was gone. Black blood streaked across the grass where his body had lain. Had he come back to life and walked off on his own or had the Australian medics taken him away—I do not know. I didn't mean to kill him. I had committed a killing,

Finger Bone

yet I did not intend it. Just as he'd stared blankly at me with his blue eyes, I'd blankly pulled the trigger. As I ran frantically from the black hunters, I lost my footing, tumbled down the slope, and lost consciousness.

When I came to, I was lying by the side of a river. My uniform and hands were caked with red clay. There was a deep gash on my forehead, but the blood had mostly coagulated. I brought myself to an upright position and glimpsed a tree rising up. It was the color of blood. With the dark blue sky at its back, the enormous blood tree loomed over me. I'd heard something about this species once before. A veteran soldier at the Buna garrison had told me about an eerie species of tree with crimson flowers called the bougainvillea. I was certain that was the species before me. Looking up at it, however, I questioned whether it was a bougainvillea. The day after we made land at Buna, I encountered the body of a Japanese soldier shot up by a Curtiss fighter. The first dead body of the war that I witnessed. It was riddled with about fifty or sixty bullets, bleeding out of every hole, staining the pavement. It appeared as if the soldier was bathing in a pool of blood. This was the image that floated to mind, as I stared at the crimson-flowered tree. The bunches of flowers resembled blood-soaked corpses hanging from the branches like crucifixions. How did such a tree exist in this world?

And then, I noticed blood spatters on the pebbles beneath the tree. Could it be the flowers were bleeding? Beyond the flowers, I noticed several branches sagging unnaturally under the weight of something. Or, was I hallucinating from malnutrition? The severed heads of Japanese soldiers were hanging from vines wrapped around their necks. Their faces were painted with red and black spots, their eyes and mouths sewed shut with crude thread, wooden spikes skewered through the bridges of their noses. Human hides hung on the branches like laundry. I quietly backed away from the tree. Then, an alluring bird cry came from the jungle. I wiped my face on my sleeve and searched overhead. The bird cry echoed and faded. I broke out in a cold sweat and retreated into the jungle, using my bayonet as a crutch. I wandered the jungle for days before I was reunited with the other invalid soldiers.

By then, I was showing signs of starvation. My trousers slipped incessantly off my hips, bones I'd never seen before sticking out from my body. There were only poisonous plants and "electric" potatoes to be found in the area. One soldier tried a potato, was seized with convulsions, and died, clawing the ground for dear life. Another ate a plant and died, foaming green at the mouth. We took to trading items for food. The irony that the cigarettes that I'd gotten from Furuya and the tooth powder I'd gotten from Shimizu bought me a couple more days of life was not lost on me. I traded the cigarettes for a bit of rock sugar. The tooth powder turned into half a cob of corn. I wondered why anyone would need to brush their teeth under the circumstances. "Well, my mess tin got stolen, you see, and I got dysentery, so the corn is only going to kill me." In other words, he intended to use the can the tooth powder came in to boil himself some rice water. I managed to elude death for several days with the food items I'd traded for. As I think back now, that was when I'd endured the worst of the hunger pains. My stomach was crawling with bugs. They clung to my insides and festered, stripping me of discipline not only as a soldier but as a human too.

One moonlit night, a soldier made a dying wish, "Send my wife and kid my love. Make sure they get a lock of my hair or my bones, doesn't matter which." Several of the soldiers prayed. Someone cut off a finger from the dead body, and someone built a fire. "We'll deliver your bones to your wife, sure we will, rest in peace," someone muttered, bringing the others to tears. No doubt they were thinking about their own wives and children. But when the finger was tossed onto the fire, the mood changed. The men's faces glowed over the flame. Their eyes, pooling with red tears, were lit with want as the smell wafted about them. I watched the men gathered around the fire from afar, dizzy from the smell. One of the soldiers used two twigs like chopsticks and pulled the finger out of the fire. No one said a word. I said not a word. He set the steaming finger on a flat white rock. The finger was reddish brown, the same as if you'd cooked beef or pork. Aside from the nail, it could've been mistaken for a meat roll or something similar. Red juices and clear fat dripped from the surface, spreading a black stain across the rock. The cork in my head began to loosen. It loosened, little by little, dizzying my senses. "We'll deliver your bones to your wife." A soldier cut off the remaining four fingers and tossed them in the fire. No one said a word. I said not a word. Nothing in the regulations stipulated that the bones of only one finger was to be delivered to the family. The smell of meat, unmistakable and brutal, filled the air. The smell was so intense that it pushed me back on my heels. Dried leaves crunched beneath my boots. That choice split our fates. I broke into a run, stumbled, and ran through the jungle until I was gasping for breath and fell unconscious. As I think on it now, this was how the cannibalism began.

Sometime later, I came onto the yellow road.

The jungle spread out on the left side of the road. It was ridden with aggressive vine plants. The vines carpeted the ground, wrapped around trees, and sprawled over the

Finger Bone

vegetation. Weakened soldiers entering the jungle in search of water got tangled in the yellowish green vines and died, unable to free themselves. If you were able to cut through the jungle, an enormous expanse of marshlands was beyond it. If you got ankle-deep in the mud, you were stuck. I happened upon the backs of dead soldiers sticking out from the murk. They might have died drinking the stagnant water.

The right side of the road was a vast desert spreading to the foothills in the distance. The vegetation was shriveled, the trees decayed. On occasion, a dead tree resembling a white birch lay in the desert plains. From afar, it looked like a human skeleton. Bounded by the jungle and desert, the yellow road stretched endlessly beyond the horizon. It might have been a vehicle road built by the Allied forces. If that were the case, then it was too dangerous to walk. An American jeep might rumble up, machine guns blazing, and mow us down. The small-caliber bullets might put hundreds of holes in my body. Neither jeep nor truck appeared. From the western sky overlooking the desert, we were completely exposed on the road. However, neither Curtiss, nor Lockheed, nor Grumman came to lay waste to our escape route.

Some stragglers fell in line with the others walking the road. Weakened soldiers stumbled and staggered, moaning, "Salamaua … Salamaua …" Some began to hum a popular military song. Their voices were labored and lacked melody. But by some fluke, from the breathless moans emerged a tune. Hearing it took my breath. It took everyone's breath. Perhaps that was the power residing in the song. A grenade exploded. Every time the song was sung to the end, another grenade exploded such that it sounded like applause. Here and there, the last line of the song was heard. Here and there, the sound of applause erupted.

One time, a twin-engine American aircraft circled the sky and began to descend toward us. I felt a sense of relief, believing the end was near. But the aircraft descended only slightly, then took off. I spotted several parachutes in the sky. They were pastel colored, like the colors of a woman's parasol. A cylinder of some kind was attached to them. The parachutes got caught in the trees, not one finding ground. One of the cylinders exploded in every direction, igniting the pastel-color parachute in flames. It was a time bomb made to look like a food can. I couldn't understand it. No soldier was going to be fooled by such a suspicious looking drop. More explosions rang out in the trees, burning the parachutes to the ground. The echoes failed even to sound like ridicule. I didn't understand it.

Sometime later, I felt a pain around my abdomen. I pulled up my shirt to find a rash around my navel, and more on the

Finger Bone

triceps, the back of the thighs, and other soft areas of my skin. The lesions were reddish black at their center; the surrounding areas were red with swollen bumps and tiny fissures penetrating the healthy skin. The next day, I came down with fever, my joints ached. I had contracted a local disease. Whether the rash was caused by dengue fever or by the mysterious killer disease, I did not know. It didn't matter. At times, the red splotches appeared to be holding hands. One lesion took a second lesion's hand, while the second lesion took another lesion's hand, killing the healthy skin a little at a time. Though the hunger pains were gone, I was thirsty. I'd drunk the water I'd collected from the creek, and my canteen was empty. If I went into the jungle to fill it, I would fall prey to the vine plants.

The flies traveled on the road along with us. The flies in the south were larger than those in Japan. Their silver-spotted legs were long, their green abdomens plump. For this reason perhaps, the maggots were also enormous. The species found on the island grew to the size of long grain rice. One soldier's thigh, where the flesh had been gouged out, was crawling with maggots as if someone had poured them with a ladle. There was something mentally rattling about seeing the white larvae wriggling inside a live man's leg. My head spun at seeing the maggots infesting a living human rather than a corpse. I felt sick to my stomach, but having nothing to vomit, the gastric acids just lingered at my throat. The soldier, however, made no attempt to remove them. He explained he was letting the maggots eat the infected parts. "Once they're done eating up the rotten flesh, I'm going to steam 'em in my mess tin and eat 'em," he said, his eyes lighting up like a child's.

I happened upon a bloated corpse lying by the side of the road. Corpses swelled. Not all of them, but a great many did. It was a fact I did not know until I'd come upon the road. The emaciated body swelled to the size of a sumo wrestler until the skin burst open. The eyes, the tongue, the bowels—every organ inside the body liquefied and dribbled out from the ruptures in the skin. A horrible odor filled the air, spoiling everything around it. An acidic smell stung the eyes. I sensed a hint of sweetness in it. As my pores breathed in the stench, my body began to emit the same odor and sweetness. Soon, I grew accustomed to the smell of death. The bloated corpses became commonplace. I no longer felt anything. Had I finally gone mad like the others? The soldiers marching around me had also grown accustomed to the bloated corpses. I suppose that was how humans were built.

Was this war? When I left the field hospital, I'd expected to be thrown back into the war. Yet, here we were marching

Finger Bone

the yellow road, mostly unarmed, without rifles or grenades, and for those whose boots had lost their heels, barefoot. Enemy aircraft flew past us, leaving us to die and rot one by one without so much as a fight. This is war, I intoned. This too is war. And for as many times as I mumbled the words to myself, they did not sink in. It was not some recitation like having to memorize the Imperial Rescript back on the base in Japan. I'd said it aloud, believing it to be true, yet in my fevered state the words did not sound like my own.

We marched and marched, yet the yellow road continued without end.

The jungle expanse, the desert plains, humans in decay, corpses turning to skeletons. The clouds floating above the plains were still, as was everything else in the dark blue sky. The unchanging landscape stretched on and on. A fixed landscape. Only the husks of men and black shadows dragged themselves across it.

I came upon a Japanese soldier sitting beneath a tree. A bloated Japanese soldier. His hands and arms stuck out straight like rods, his insides swollen and devoured by maggots, a gray tar-like excretion oozing out of the ruptured skin. The right eye was protruding halfway out of the socket, while the left eye had fallen out completely, dangling on the chest. Sinews—or was it nerves or muscles—hung out of the socket, barely attached to the eye. Maggots stuck to the sinews like grains of rice; it was only a matter of time before the eye would fall on the grass.

For days, I marched without food or water. And then, I happened upon the bloated corpse again. Or, it might have been a different soldier's corpse. The right eye spilling halfway out of the socket and the dangling left eye were the same as the one before. Perhaps the road did not lead anywhere. Perhaps we were merely going around in circles, like tracing the edge of an enormous hole. When the bloated corpse appeared for a third time, I stopped.

I broke from the yellow road and decided to take a rest beneath a tree by the roadside. The tree resembled a zelkova. I leaned back against the trunk and lowered myself to the ground. When my buttocks nestled between the roots, I knew I would not have the strength to stand. I lacked the means to take my own life. I had neither rifle nor grenade in my possession. The bayonet I'd been using as a cane had broken some time ago. And so, I waited for death to take me.

I knew why Sergeant Tanabe had volunteered for a mission to certain death. He had predicted the supplies would stall and the Japanese forces would eventually retreat; he'd recognized the battle of Isurava would be a fitting burial ground for a warrior. "We do not fight to die," Sergeant

Finger Bone

Tanabe had said some time ago. "We do not fight to die. We fight to win. If we die, there is no winning or losing. We must think only of surviving in whatever difficulty we find ourselves." Perhaps what Sergeant Tanabe had meant by "win" was "overcome." And then, a fire was kindled inside me. It was as intense as candlelight. If I truly intended to kill myself, I did not require a pistol or a grenade. I needed only to bite off my tongue. Resting my head on the trunk with my chin tilted up, I pushed the tongue against the inside of my lips. To overcome. I clamped the surprisingly meaty base between my teeth. I bit down with everything I could muster. You can't help open your eyes wide in moments like these. I bit down harder. And then, the warm, soft, thick meat gave way against my teeth. Sadly, it made me hungry. It was impossible to bite off your tongue when you were hungry. I felt the tongue swell with blood, and unable to retract it, an emotion crept up from within. I'd expected to laugh it off, but what came next were tears. They dried quickly in the tropical sun. Leaning against the tree, I gazed at the husks of men shambling past, with my tongue sticking lazily out of my mouth, streaks of salt chalking my cheeks. Peel back the layers and you were a cannibal. Peel back the layers and you were a killer. Peel back my layers and this was what I was revealed to be.

"Hey, what unit are you with?"

There was a black shadow standing over me. I could not answer. The shadow crouched down, muttering, "Go on then," and went on its way. Sometime later, I noticed the grenade lying where the soldier had crouched. I stared at it. The belly of the grenade was sweating in the hot sun. I pulled my tongue back and took the cylinder in my hand. The sun was slanting toward the foothills, which meant that half the day had passed.

The sky in the west was crimson.

The bleeding sun leaned toward the ridgeline. Though the sun appeared still, instant by instant, it moved. With every instant, it poured forth a scene that might never be seen again. The end of the day. The brief period when your shadow was longest. Exerting the last of its strength, my shadow cast shade across the yellow road, until it broke from my feet.

Every few seconds, my view was overtaken by darkness. I realized shortly after that it was just my eyes blinking. Perhaps because of the translucence of my eyelids, several rainbows floated in the dark. The arches waved left and right, leaving a light trail as they drew closer. If I passed through those arches, I knew there would be no coming back. As I readied to go under the curves of the rainbow, my eyes labored open, filling me with the colors of the sunset. And then, my thoughts returned to the finger bone.

Finger Bone

Before I departed Field Hospital No. 3, I'd stored Sanada's finger bone and ID tag in an aluminum bento box and tucked it inside my rucksack. The aluminum would not decompose; it would long outlast my bones. Someday the war would be over. Decades from now, someone might eventually find the bento box and deliver it to Kotaro. That was my wager and my struggle. My struggle against life, or against fate, or against the war that I'd been thrown into. I'd lost my ID tag and Chizuru's good-luck satchel somewhere in the jungle. If I became a skeleton, no one would know who I was.

I tried to imagine the day the finger bone would be delivered. Decades on, on a hot August day, the bone would be delivered to Kotaro. The boy who used to toddle about holding onto the edge of the low table would be a man. Fanning himself with a paper fan, he is drinking cold barley tea in the living room. Rattling the ice in the glass. His wife is sitting across from him at the table, fanning her chest. The cicadas chirring in the trees pause for a moment, then pick up again. It is a summer evening. And then, someone opens the sliding door at the entrance and announces himself, "Hello, may I come in?" His wife is holding the newborn, so Kotaro puts on his slippers and goes out to the hall. Then, the deliverer of the bone removes the aluminum lid and says, "A brave soldier perished in the line of duty while attempting to deliver your father's bone. I hope you will honor him by burning incense at your father's altar."

Imagining it felt like a cool drink of water.

When my eyes opened next, my field of vision was sideways. It appeared as if the world had fallen on its side, but it was my body that had. The grenade pin may have come loose in the fall.

There was an arm of a corpse lying in the setting sun. The fingers were curved inward as if they were holding an egg. From my sideways view of the world, I stared somewhat curiously at the hand gripping something with care.

Afterword

SOME TIME AGO, I tasted a fruit I did not recognize at a Kanaka village. One of the young men I'd gotten to know offered me a yellow-green fruit resembling a papaya. He explained it was eaten with the white powder of crushed coral sprinkled on top. I took a bite, and my head spun violently as if I'd downed a strong drink. The blood vessels in my body expanded, and my body began to burn. I noticed the young man eating the fruit had blood all around his mouth. His lips, his teeth, his gums were glistening red. Suddenly, the saliva pooled under my tongue, and I spat it out on the ground. It too was the color of blood. I shook my head and handed the fruit back to him. He smiled, flashing his red teeth, and took another bite of the fruit. I smiled back. I realize now that the fruit likely had effects similar to those of opium.

honfordstar.com